Bríd

by

Mary McAlinden

Chapter 1

It was a cold winters morning with frost glistening on the roads. The people of Dunclare were starting to rouse from their sleep, for the beginning of a brand-new day.

Dunclare is a sleepy little village in Co. Roscommon in the west of Ireland. The people of Dunclare were so proud that they could boast of their very own church, St Patricks. Standing next to it was a school where all the children from the village and surrounding farms attended.

The school building was also used as the parish dance hall. Folk would travel from miles around for the monthly dance. It was at these dances that the young people met and from where most of the romances would spring.

The village consisted of only eight houses, so of course, everyone knew each other. After the dance, tongues would start wagging, as they all knew who had taken which girl home. It was tough trying to keep anything quiet.

Also, in the village was a post office and a general store. Ryan's store sold almost everything it was also the grocers, butchers, drapers and even the local pub. If larger items were required folk would have to travel to Derrytagh, a small market town three miles away down the Elphin Road. Ryan's store always had a distinctive aroma. It was a mixture of all kinds of food and drink, also with a strong smell of paraffin that was used for oil lamps to light up the people's homes.

Fresh creamy milk, butter and eggs would be purchased from the local farms.

There was only one 'well' from which all the residents drew their lovely clear spring water.

There was very little work in the area, apart from labouring jobs on the farms, but they were mostly seasonal. Most of the young men when they reached their teens would leave their homes to seek work in either England, Scotland or America. Relatives who had emigrated earlier would send them their fares.

The girls when they were old enough went off to Dublin, Galway or Cork to work as maids in hotels or the big houses of the Gentry.

The nearest police barracks was in Elphin, a small town two miles away as there was very little or no need for one in this quiet and peaceful village of Dunclare. John Donnelly was the police sergeant in Elphin, but he and his wife Maggie and family lived in Dunclare

One icy cold morning Sgt. Donnelly was nearing his home after working the night shift. It was almost 6 am and the Donnelly household would soon be waking from their slumbers. "Bridie are you out of bed yet?" John Donnelly shouted from the bottom of the stairs. The loud voice of her father made Bridie wake with a start. John Donnelly was a giant of a man with a mop of red hair that matched his temper. He often threatened the children with his broad leather belt. John hated his job, but with a large family to feed, there was no choice. He was always sorry after shouting at the children but would never lift his hand to any of them. He prayed every night that his lovely country would be free and that the Irish would be left to run their land.

Bridie jumped out of bed, trying not to disturb her sisters with whom she shared a bed. Her sleepy eyes went straight toward the small window in the far corner of the bedroom; she could see that it was still dark outside.

"I hate these cold dark mornings", Bridie thought as she blessed herself then saying her morning prayers while at the same time swiftly putting on her black shift dress. As Bridie went quickly but quietly down the bare wooden stairs, she shivered with the cold, then reluctantly stepped onto the cold stone floor in her bare feet.

The Donnelly house had a big open turf fire where all the cooking was done, and Bridie soon had it alight. She made a big pan of porridge and gave her father his. She left the pan warming for the children when they got up for school later. While her father was eating his breakfast, Bridie took a cup of tea into her mother. Her parents slept downstairs in the parlour as there were only two bedrooms upstairs.

Maggie Donnelly had given birth to baby Bernadette the day before, or she would have been up herself attending to her family. "Thank you, Achushla", Maggie said to her young daughter, "I don't know what I would do without you, God bless you, darling child". Maggie Donnelly was a homely quiet-spoken woman. As the local midwife she had brought most of the local children into the world and was highly respected by everyone in and around the village, Although she had not worked for some length of time, folk would still call upon her for help and advice.

Bridie looked at her mother's pale face and held back her tears. She hated to see her mother look so unwell. "You stay in bed, Mama. I will wash and change the baby", she said. Maggie felt a sense of guilt as she looked up at her young daughter, but she was so weak after this baby, her eighth child. Even though Maggie loved all her children dearly and would not be without them for the world, she prayed with all her heart that this new-born child would be her last. Bridie was her eldest daughter, so she had to rely on her for so much help even though she was only eleven years of age.

It saddened Maggie greatly that Bridie had so much to do, as she laid her weary head back onto her pillow thinking of her daughter who was only a child herself, yet with the responsibilities of a grown woman. Bridie bent down and lifted her new baby sister out of her mother's bed, gave her a gentle little kiss then cradled her in her small arms. As Bridie was walking back into the kitchen her father pushed passed her on his way to bed saying, "Keep that child quiet I have had a hard, tiring night, and I need my sleep". Thank God he is going straight to bed thought Bridie as he was always in a bad mood in the mornings, the family tried to keep out of his way.

After the baby was washed and changed Bridie wrapped her in a shawl then laid her in the small cradle near the fireside, then she made herself a cup of tea. Bridie sat on a stool looking into the flames of the fire as she added a couple more sods of turf thinking of how she loved her mother so much and knew her mother needed all the help she could give her. She wished that she too could go to school as she missed seeing all her friends. She also preferred doing essays and times tables than cooking, cleaning and looking after the family.

Bridie loved school; it was a small school with one room divided by a folding door that opened and closed like a concertina. Mr Smyth, the headmaster, taught the older children while Miss Murphy taught the younger ones. Mr Smyth was a very understanding person who had given permission for Bridie to have two weeks leave to help her mother. He would say that Bridie would have no problem catching up with her studies when she returned as she was his star pupil. Mr Smyth had told John and Maggie that their daughter was a very bright girl with a good head on her shoulders and that she would make a good schoolteacher herself one day.

Bridie was aroused from her daydreaming by her older brother Tom as he came down the stairs with little Annie in his arms. It was about time that they were all up, so Bridie went up to arouse them. There was Danny, Geraldine, Kathleen and Margaret to get ready for school. They were all warned to be quiet and not to make any noise when they went downstairs. There was no need for Bridie to worry about the children disturbing their father this morning as it was far too cold for them to fool around. They all huddled around the fire making feeble excuses to stay off school. Then after breakfast, they all washed in the same basin of water that Tom had put on a chair close to the fire, then the older children got ready for school. Bridie sighed with relief as she watched them run up the road to school, laughing and shouting to their friends as they went. Mr Ryan was stacking boxes of vegetables outside his shop window, which was straight opposite the Donnelly house. He waved over to Bridie said good morning then asked how her mother and baby were. Bridie had a few words with him then went back into the house to take care of the younger children.

It only took Maggie a few more days then she was back

taking care of her young family again. "Bridie", said Maggie, "Before you go back to school, we will have a day out in Derrytagh just the two of us. Mrs Moffatt said she would take care of the children for me". Bridie was delighted, for she knew this was a special treat for her. It would also be lovely having a day out with her mother, just the two of them together.

Thursday was 'Fair day' in Derrytagh, and there was always someone from the village going, so it was easy enough to get a lift whether it be in a pony and trap or horse and cart. The farmers would take their cattle while the tinkers would take their horses so a lot of buying and selling would take place. After the conclusion of business, the farmers would go into the pubs for a few 'jars'. The farmers had worked hard all week, and 'Fair day' was a time to relax and to meet up with friends and relations. It was something to look forward to each week. Maggie and Bridie were being taken to the fair by Bryan and Clare Gaffney in their pony and trap. They were a middle-aged couple but sadly were childless, so they were very set in their ways, but Maggie had always found them to be very nice.

Thursday came, and Bridie helped her mother with the children, firstly taking the older ones to school and then on to Mrs Moffatt's with the younger children. The Gaffney's came right on time, Maggie and Bridie were ready for them. When they got into the trap, Clare put a woollen blanket over Maggie's knees, but Maggie made sure that Bridie had a share of it too. They arrived in Derrytagh a small bustling town just after mid-day, Bryan helped Maggie and Bridie down from the trap while informing them that he would pick them up outside Kelly's shoe shop in the centre of town at two-thirty to return home. It was a lovely bright sunny day but quite cold so Maggie suggested to her daughter that they should call into O'Brien's tearoom for a hot cup of tea and a treacle scone.

Although Derrytagh was a small town with only one main street, it had some lovely shops, so Maggie and Bridie were enjoying every minute window shopping while buying a few odds and ends not forgetting sweets for the children. Also, as a special treat, they went into Cafola's Ice Cream Parlour for delicious ice cream with chocolate sprinkled on top. It had been a wonderful day. It was hard to tell who had enjoyed it the most. Bridie was so happy to see her mother laughing and joking with friends they had met in town before they made their way to meet the Gaffney's for their journey back home.

Before long, everything in the Donnelly household was back to normal. The baby was thriving well. The rest of the children were all getting excited talking about Father Christmas. They helped their mother to make decorations to hang over the fireplace and sat listening to their mother telling fascinating stories about the fairies who help Father Christmas make the presents.

It was three weeks before Christmas when Bridie awoke to hear voices coming from downstairs. Then she was sure she heard someone crying. She crept out of bed, dressed, then slowly walked down the stairs, afraid of what she would find. She saw her mother was sitting cradling young Annie in her arms with her father standing at her side and Doctor Healy putting on his coat. Maggie looked up at Bridie the tears falling down her pale face, and Bridie realised something awful must have happened. She looked at Doctor Healy as he came walking toward her, he laid his hand on her shoulder and said softly, "Your sister Annie has died of pneumonia, make your mother and father a strong cup of tea there's a good girl". The tears welled up in Bridie's eyes. She must be dreaming; Annie was only two years of age. She knew Annie had a cold but surely you do not die with a cold! Her father took Annie out of her mother's arms and walked with her into their bedroom, and then Bridie ran into her mother's outstretched arms where they clung to each other sobbing.

The whole family were broken-hearted over the death of little Annie but as it was nearing Christmas and although Maggie was grieving over the loss of her darling child, she tried her best to hide her grief from the children. She kept on telling herself that her young girl was in heaven, had not Father Lynch told her so anyway. Maggie would sit at night after John had gone off to his work and the family all tucked up in bed, knitting jumpers and socks for her children as she wanted all of them to look smart on Christmas morning when they all went to mass.

It started to snow on Christmas Eve, all the children in the village were having a great time playing in the snow and trying to catch the big soft snowflakes that were floating down from the skies. When it was time for them to come in, Maggie had a mug of hot milk and a piece of soda bread and butter ready for them which they ate with relish after being out in the cold. As they all sat around the lovely big turf fire, Maggie looked lovingly at her beautiful children and thought how lucky she was to have them but her heart was still aching so much for her darling baby that she had lost. All the children were tired out after playing out in the cold night air and were soon tucked up in their beds. As Maggie had just settled herself at the fire to read a book

'The Ramblers' started to call, they knew there would be no music or singing in the Donnelly household for quite a while, so they were all away long before midnight, letting Bridie know she had their support in her grief. 'The Ramblers' were neighbours and men around the village who would gather in different houses for the craic and a sing-song. Some would bring their fiddles and tin whistles so they could have a dance in the kitchen. Someone would shout "round the house" and "mind the dresser" and, the set dancing would begin. Everyone always had a great time. The Ramblers loved going to the Donnelly's as Maggie was a great storyteller; they often stayed until the wee small hours. Some of the young men would be afraid of going home in the dark after listening to all the ghost stories, but they would all be back for more the following week.

Chapter 2

Christmas day came and went, the snow had rapidly disappeared as quickly as it had come, but the mornings were still cold and frosty. The day after New Year's Day Bridie went to Galway to stay with her Aunt Rosie for a few days as a special treat for her. Rosie Lavery was Maggie's only sister. She had never married and always said that she liked her independence too much and would not have any man telling her how to run her life. Rosie had worked as head cook for a well-to-do family called Cass for over ten years. They lived in Salthill in a big house overlooking the bay. Her quarters were at the top of the house. Rosie enjoyed her job as she loved cooking. The Cass family had been very good to her over the years, making her feel part of their family. Next month Rosie would be emigrating to America, she had been saving for years to make her dream come true and now please God if all goes according to plan she would be in Chicago in a few weeks.

Rosie was all smiles as she met Bridie off the bus. "Hello me darlin, how's my girl then?" she asked her niece taking hold of her hand and taking the small parcel that Bridie had under her arm. Bridie loved these trips to her aunt. She had been here once before and was quite excited about her holiday. Rosie knew that much of Bridie's young life was spent in helping her mother to take care of the children, so she was going to make the next few days extra special for her young niece. Rosie took Bridie sight-seeing; they even went to the theatre where Ireland's top artists appeared. At night they would go for walks along the golden beach, the fresh breeze from the ocean always gave them an appetite, but Rose would soon have them a lovely hot meal when they returned to the house.

Bridie shared her aunt's lovely big feather bed so they would talk and laugh until one or the other would drop off to sleep. Little problems that Bridie may have had she would confide them to her aunt because she had plenty of time to sit and listen. She wished she could talk to her mother in the same way, but Bridie knew her dear mother was always washing, baking bread and cooking, ever surrounded by children.

The few days that Bridie spent in Galway would remain in her memory forever. She had enjoyed every minute, but they had gone over far too quickly, and she felt sad that this would probably be the last time she would ever spend with her aunt Rosie. As the bus was coming in Rosie hid her tears from her young niece saying, as she gave her a great big hug, "Now be off with you darlin, give my regards to all the family. Tell your mother I will write to her as soon as I am settled in Chicago". Then, handing Bridie a cardboard box, helped her onto the bus. Bridie held onto the box as if it were gold, and she knew what was in it, there was home-cooked pies, jars of jam, cakes also chocolate and sweets for the children.

As the bus made its way along the winding country roads on the journey to Dunclare, Bridie started to get excited at the thought of seeing her mother and family again even though she was sad at leaving aunt Rose. The bus seemed to be taking forever with the driver chatting to everyone as if he had all the time in the world. People would also stop the bus and ask the driver to drop off a parcel at someone's house, which he did quite happily.

At last, the bus was nearing home Bridie could see her brothers and sisters jumping up and down as they waited for her hoping that she had something for them. Standing looking over the half-door was her darling mother with the baby wrapped in a shawl. The bus driver helped Bridie off the bus with her precious box. She was the only one to get off at the village. "Sure you are a lucky girl having a welcoming party waiting for you," the bus driver said to Bridie with his lovely smile lighting up his handsome face, then he waved goodbye as he drove the bus away.

Maggie thought how grown up her daughter looked as she opened the door walking toward her. "Hello, Mama, is everyone well?" asked Bridie as she struggled with the box of goodies. "Tom", said Maggie, "Take that box from your sister can't you see it's heavy", as all the children were dancing around Bridie. "You look lovely and healthy," Maggie said, "the sea air has done you a power of good but come on child take off your coat, we will have our tea then you can tell us all about your holiday".

Maggie had the table set, the kettle boiling away over the fire ready to make the tea and John Donnelly was sitting on a stool by the fireside polishing the children's shoes for school the next day. John never helped with housework or the children as he, like most men, thought that was woman's work, but the one thing he did was to polish all the shoes as he wanted his children looking smart. He had a reputation to keep up, seeing that he was the local police sergeant.

"Have you had a good holiday darlin?" John said to his daughter as he stood up, taking the box from Tom with the children all crowding around him, eager to see what aunt Rosie had sent them. "Yes, Da Da" replied Bridie warming her hands at the fire. "I had a lovely time, and Aunt Rosie sends her love to everyone."

Over tea, Bridie told her eager listeners all about her stay in Galway then winking to her mother added a few make-believe tales to the children. She was getting her mother's devilish sense of humour that many Irish people have. After tea, Maggie told her children it was time to have their hair washed as the water was now hot enough after heating in a three-legged pot over the fire. Rainwater collected in a big wooden barrel that always stood outside the back door. It was this water that was heated to wash the hair and kept it in good condition. Folk would comment on the girls' hair as it had a sheen on it just like silk. Their hair was down to their waist, so it took a long time for it to dry with only the heat of the fire to dry it. Later in the evening, John said goodbye to his wife and children before going to work, and then Maggie made them all a cup of hot milk and one of Aunt Rosie's biscuits before they all retired for an early night.

The Christmas and New Year holidays were now long past, and Bridie noticed that the mornings were now starting to get lighter. It was no longer dark outside when she looked towards the bedroom window when her father shouted up the stairs for her to get up. Maggie, of course, was always up and would have all the children's clothes warming beside the fire, she would also have the porridge made. One morning as soon as breakfast was over Maggie said to her son Tom, "Before you go off to school Tom I want you to go and ask Doctor Healy if he will come to have a look at the baby. Tell him that she is very chesty, she also has a high temperature and that I am quite worried about her". Without another word, Tom put on his coat and ran the mile to the doctor's house and was out of breath when he arrived. The doctor could only make out part of what Tom was blurting out to him. "I think you had better come into the parlour me lad", the doctor said, "Now sit down there Tom and start again slowly". Tom repeated more clearly what his mother had told him to say. "Well me boyo", Doctor Healy said, "I will be ready in two shakes of a donkey's tail, you can ride back with me into the village."

Bridie crept into her parent's bedroom to see her baby sister before she went off to school, she is a lovely baby thought Bridie as she bent down and kissed her warm cheek.

Dr Healy tried his utmost to save the life of baby Bernadette, but she just could not respond to the medicine and died in Maggie's arms two days later. John and Maggie were devastated that they had lost two of their children, how much more sorrow could they bear in life.

But this was not to be the last of the Donnelly's grief for on Easter Saturday only three weeks after the death of the baby, John Donnelly died suddenly of a heart attack. Everyone said he had died of a broken heart as he could not get over the loss of his babies. Although John appeared a hard man at times, he dearly loved his wife and children, they all knew this, and they all loved him in return.

Maggie was broken-hearted, "What have I done to deserve all this sorrow", she cried as she was still mourning the loss of her two children. The rest of the Donnelly children were all confused and afraid as they clung to each other crying, "What will we do without Da Da", Tom said to Bridie, then he ran up the stairs crying. Mrs O'Boyle and Mrs Moffatt were there to see what help they could be to Maggie and the family.

Bridie was listening to everyone talking and crying, and she could not take anymore. She went out of the house, ran all the way up to the church, then knelt before the altar and prayed, "Please God don't let anyone else die, please God don't let my mother die".

John's body was laid out in the parlour, and as it was an Easter weekend, the funeral would take place on Tuesday, the wake would last for three days and nights. In Ireland you automatically had a wake when someone died. Relatives, friends and neighbours would come from near and far to pay their respect. The rosary would be said, and people would kneel at the coffin to say their own private prayers. A lot of the men would have a drink. They would talk about the weather, how many cattle they had or whether they would have good crops that year. Then after a few drinks, the stories would start. A lot of the men were really gifted and could tell a good yarn, and this helped to keep the family's mind off their grieving for a while. Of course, the men loved a wake as it was a chance for a get-together.

Tuesday came, the funeral had taken place so now Maggie and her children would have to get on with their lives as best they could. Before the week was over, Maggie realised that times were going to change dramatically. She knew that hard times were ahead for the family. At that time Ireland was under British Rule, and John had worked in the Royal Irish Constabulary. Maggie received a letter from them stating that even though John had been a sergeant, she was not entitled to any pension or help with the funeral expenses. Their excuse was he had not been in the force long enough to qualify.

"What am I going to do? How am I going to feed and

clothe six children with no money coming in?" Maggie said to Father Noel Lynch as they sat talking in the kitchen. Father Lynch tried to be helpful and console Maggie, but he knew there was little he could do to lessen her burden as he himself like most of his parishioners were just scraping a living themselves. As they sat talking, there came a quiet tap at the front door. Maggie was surprised to see that it was Mrs Carey, the postmistress. "Hello Mrs Carey, won't you please come in?" Maggie said, holding open the door for her. Mrs Carey exchanged greetings with Father Lynch then turning to Maggie said, "I am sorry to intrude Mrs Donnelly, but I have just come to tell you that Paull Gaffney our postman is leaving, he is going off to America". Maggie was quite pleased with what Mrs Carey was telling her. "Won't you sit down Mrs Carey you are welcome to a cup of tea", Maggie said, still very puzzled.

"I won't if you don't mind Mrs Donnelly, as I have to get back to the post office. What I have come to tell you is, that when Paul leaves his post round, we will need someone to take his place". Mrs Carey then gave a small pause before continuing to say, "Your late husband gave Mr Carey and myself a lot of help and assistance over the years, for which we were always very grateful. In return, we would like to offer young Tom the job as postman". Maggie looked from Mrs Carey to Father Lynch in utter amazement. "But he is still at school, and he is only thirteen years of age", she said. Father Lynch stood up, then taking hold of Maggie's hands said, "Sure the boy will be leaving at the end of the year now, won't he? Leave everything to me, Maggie, do not you worry about anything. I will get permission for Tom to leave school, and I am sure there won't be any problem".

It was only two weeks later that Tom started his job as the local postman. Tom loved his job and felt very proud that he was helping his mother, as the small amount of money he earned was a godsend to the family. Tom though, would be very tired when he came home from work as he had to walk for miles to out-lying cottages and farms with the letters. He was made to feel very welcome when he delivered the mail as a lot of it would contain money from relatives who had left home to work in another country. All his customers offered him cups of tea or milk.

The post-mistress Mrs Carey was very pleased with Tom's work as he was always punctual and folk commented to her what a nice mannered boy he was, also that he always had a cheery word for them. Tom was delighted when Mrs Carey bought him a second-hand bicycle, so it made his deliveries that much quicker.

Maggie was relieved that Tom liked his job as she was always worried that he might be tempted to join the British Army. The Army would go around the towns and villages trying to persuade the young men to join up. Written on the side of the Army van was a verse about an Irishman, who had been awarded the Victoria Cross for his bravery:

Arragh Glory Mike O'Leary

You're the grandest boy of all

Sure there's not an Irish Colleen

From Macroon to Donegal

That are proud of you and prouder

Than a peacock of its tail

Arragh Glory Mike O'Leary

You're the pride of Inishfail

The children in the village would dance around the van singing the verse about Mike O'Leary making up their own tune for it. The rest of the villagers would be behind closed doors ignoring the Army's plea.

Bridie was now earning a few pennies helping on O'Brien's farm when needed, and once a week she would babysit for them. As the farm was quite a distance from home Bridie would stay there on a Saturday night as it was too dark and late for her to go home, then she would get a lift home by Mary O'Brien. The children were aged four, three and one years old, and Bridie enjoyed looking after them as they were lovely children. When they were in bed Bridie would sit and read a book until the O'Brien's came home, then she would go to bed sleeping in the spare bedroom.

On one occasion Mike arrived home early on his own saying that he did not feel well, and a friend would be bringing his wife home later. Bridie was not sure what to do, will I go to bed she thought, but she felt uncomfortable with Mrs O'Brien not there, and she could see that he had been drinking too much. He sat on the arm of the chair beside Bridie, he put his arm around her small waist and asked her if she had a boyfriend. Bridie was sensible enough to know that what he was doing and saying was wrong, so she picked up her coat saying she was going home, then ran out of the house. As it was night-time, Bridie was terrified going home along the dark, isolated country lanes, so she started to run. When Bridie was almost halfway home, she thought she heard a noise. She stood quite still for a moment, then she heard it again. It was the sound of chains rattling. It must be the devil, she thought, as she stood terrified in the dark. What shall I do she asked herself shaking with fear, but she knew she had to go on, she could not go back. Bridie made the sign of the cross then slowly walked onward her heart pounding in her chest. The rattle of the chains was getting louder, with tears falling down her cheeks, she prayed to the Virgin Mary to be at her side and protect her. As she got closer and closer to the noise, she smiled through her tears and with relief to find it was Paddy Degnan's old donkey tethered to a gate with a chain. Bridie ran all the way home regardless.

Over the next few years, life was extremely hard for the Donnelly family as it was for lots of families in Ireland at that time. The only money they had coming in was the small amount Tom earned on his post-round. With this, Maggie would buy some flour to make soda bread. They mostly lived on a few potatoes with nothing on them but a sprinkling of salt. It was a blessing that they had their own turf, so they were able to have essential heat to warm their frail bodies. Some of the men would cut the turf and bring it down from the bog then stack it up behind the back door, and this was a great help to her. Most of the people were desperately poor, but they never lost their faith or sense of humour. The Irish seemed to have music in their blood so quite often some of the men would be called upon to play a few tunes for a dance. The dances would start around ten o'clock then go on until two o'clock in the morning.

Bridie loved dancing, and she was already turning into a beautiful young woman, she had lovely dark auburn hair with a complexion any girl would envy. Many a young man's head was turned when they saw her. The first time Bridie found romance was when she was fifteen years of age, a group of travelling people with a circus were staying near the village for a couple of weeks. She met one of the young men, Michael O'Hara, when they were at the well getting water. Bridies heart gave a flutter when she saw him. He was the most handsome young man that she had ever seen. He was taller than her with very dark hair and skin, with a smile that just melted her heart. She knew she had fallen in love, and it was the most wonderful feeling in the world. They got very friendly and saw each other quite a lot, and they would go for walks over the fields hand in hand. Michael told Bridie that he was in love with her and asked her to go to Scotland with him as the circus was leaving, but Bridie knew her mother would not approve.

On the eve of Michael's departure, they clung to each other tightly, both of them broken-hearted as they said goodbye knowing that they would never see each other again. Both were vowing they would always be in their hearts forever. That night Bridie's pillow was wet with her tears for her first love as she cried herself to sleep.

It took Bridie a very long time to get over Michael. She knew in her heart, she would never forget him, but life had to go on. She would be sixteen in a few weeks and would soon have to leave home to seek work maybe in Dublin where some of her friends had already gone.

Chapter 3

Maggie received a letter one day from her brother Willy who lived in England. He had never been back to Ireland since he left at fifteen years of age to join the Merchant Navy. He was married now to a girl from Wexford with a family of his own. They had settled down in Wallsend a small town in the North East of England. Willy had said in his letter that if Bridie wanted to go over to England, she would be more than welcome to stay with him and his family. When Maggie read her brothers letter out to the family, Bridie got quite excited at the thought of going to England and getting a good job.

Bridie's thoughts went racing. She would go for six months or maybe a year and would save all the money that she would earn then come back home to take care of the family, making sure they would never go hungry again. Then she came down to earth sadly realising it was impossible, how would she ever get her fare to England. It was only a few shillings but a fortune to the Donnelly family.

Mrs Gough's whose husband was also a police sergeant would call in to see Maggie if she was passing through the village. As it happened, she called on the very day when all the family were talking about Bridie going to England to work. Mary Gough loved calling at the Donnelly's. She loved to be among the children as she was never blessed with any family of her own. The children also loved Mrs Gough to call. She always made them laugh by teasing them and making a big fuss over them. She would bring sweets for them all, but she had a big soft spot for Bridie. She would have loved a daughter just like her. After Mrs Gough finished her cup of tea and her chat with Maggie, she stood up putting on her coat saying, "I will give you your fare to England Bridie, I have a little money put away, and sure I won't be needing it for anything". Bridie's lovely brown eyes lit up as her fresh young face looked at her mother. Then Maggie with tears in her eyes said, "God bless you, Mrs Gough, you have always been a good friend to us over the years I will never forget your kindness, may God bless you."

Two weeks later, Bridie was to begin her journey to England. On the morning of her departure she was up very early to say goodbye to her brother Tom before he went on his post-round, then she walked the children up to school before saying goodbye to her mother.

Maggie stood with her precious daughter at the corner, waiting for the Dublin bus to arrive. She had already told Bridie to be careful of strangers, not to forget her morning prayers and made her promise that she would always go to Mass on Sundays and Holy Days of obligation.

As the bus was pulling in Bridie turned to her mother saying, "I will write to you as soon as I arrive at Uncle Willy's. I will send you money every week so that you will have no more worry". Then she burst into tears sobbing in her mother's arms. Tears were also falling down Maggie's face as she bade her daughter goodbye. The bus moved away slowly as most of the villagers were waving goodbye, but Bridie through her tears could only see the face of her beloved mother. All of Bridie's friends thought that she was so lucky to be going to England to work. They said it would be such an exciting experience for her, and that they couldn't wait for her to return home at Christmas to tell them all about it, but Bridie now wished it was someone else going away not her. Bridie was excited as anyone at first, but now she realised she did not want to leave home, but it was too late as everything had been arranged. So to Bridie, this was going to be a journey of sadness, not happiness.

It was a dark and misty night when the bus arrived at Dun Laoghaire harbour, and Bridie shivered in the cold night air as she stepped off the bus with her small canvas case. The lights of the boat were shining down through the mist, and people were rushing forward to get aboard. But Bridie walked steadily toward the boat, looking all around her. There was a wooden walkway with nothing but a rope on either side to hold onto, that led up to the boat. Bridie stepped on to it then froze, too terrified to go any further, "What if I fall into the water", her heart cried, "I can't swim, what will I do?".

A woman passenger who could see that Bridie was afraid took hold of her hand and guided her onto the boat. "Let's go downstairs", the woman said, still holding onto Bridie's arm. When they went downstairs, people were milling around looking for seats, so they were lucky to find two empty spaces on one of the wooden benches. Before long, the boat was full to capacity, with people having to sit on their cases or the floor. The woman introduced herself saying her name was Eileen Gallagher from Donegal. She was on her way to Nuneaton in the Midlands, to stay awhile with her sister, who had been in hospital with Tuberculosis. Bridie was so pleased she had met Eileen, she found her a very warm and caring person. They had been talking for a good while before the boat moved off, so Bridie told Eileen a little bit about herself and where she was going to. As the boat was moving out into the Irish sea, Eileen asked Bridie if she would like to go upstairs on deck for a while, but Bridie declined her offer saying that she would prefer just to stay where she was as she felt safer there. Also, she could not bear to see her beloved Isle, disappearing from view.

A young man started to play the accordion so before very long people were singing to the music. Bridie enjoyed the singing as she loved all kinds of Irish music. She was always singing or whistling herself, but tonight she could not bring herself to join in with them. She was feeling very homesick already, as some of the songs were ones that had been sung in their home on many an occasion.

The boat arrived in Holyhead Harbour early the next morning. Her companion Eileen Gallagher said for them to sit awhile until the bulk of the crowd had gone as there was no sense getting crushed. The trains would still be there when they got off. When they left the boat, Bridie thanked Eileen for her help and company on their long boat journey, and then they said goodbye as they made their way for different trains. The train that would take Bridie on her long journey to Newcastle looked quite full, but she did manage to get a seat in one of the compartments, after walking halfway down the train looking in each one, as she passed. As the train puffed its way out of the harbour, Bridie felt very tired and hungry. She took out a piece of soda bread that her mother had made for her. She tried to eat it, but tears filled her tired eyes as her thoughts wandered back home. "Oh, dear God" her heart cried out with pain. "I wish I were back with my mother. I miss her so much". But as she was so tired, it was not long before she fell asleep.

Bridie woke up when she heard someone saying, "We are nearly there, it won't be long before we are in

Newcastle". At last, the long journey was almost over, and Bridie's thoughts went to her Uncle Willy, who would be waiting at Newcastle Railway Station for her. Bridie had never met her Uncle Willy, but her mother had told her all about him. She knew he was tall and handsome, also that he was very clever as he had been all over the world serving in the Merchant Navy. As he was her only uncle, she was quite excited at meeting him, she knew that he would make her very welcome.

The train, at last, pulled into Newcastle Station, Bridie followed the surge of people towards the ticket barrier. Once outside the platform, Bridie's eyes searched the crowds of people for her Uncle Willy, her heart pounding in her chest with excitement, but she could see no one that fitted his description. Bridie put down her small suitcase and waited, "I am not going to worry", she said to herself, "I know he will be here any minute now, I will just stand here so that he will see me". Thirty-five minutes had passed as Bridie looked again at the big overpowering clock hanging in the station, by now she was getting quite frightened as her eyes searched again and again around the large, bare railway station. As she stood there, all sorts of things went racing through her mind. Had her uncle been in an accident and maybe even died as a result of it? Another few minutes had past when a very stout woman came up to her, saying, "Are you Willy's niece from Ireland?" Bridie nodded. "Well your uncle asked me to get you, seeing that I was coming to town. It would save him the fare no doubt. Hmm, is that the only bag you have with you? Well you better pick it up and hurry yourself up, as we have a long walk to get the tram to Wallsend. I have wasted enough time already". The woman went quiet, and then she started again. "I must get home as the bairns will be home from school.

God knows what they will be getting up to on their own". Then she turned her back on Bridie and started to walk away quickly. Bridie picked up her case almost running after the grumpy woman with the strange accent. As they walked along the streets for their bus, Bridie was amazed at the size of the large, grey buildings, also the crowds of people walking in the streets all of them with pale gloomy faces.

Bridie's stomach turned over wishing with all her heart that she was back home in beautiful Dunclare where the air was fresh and clean, where its people had rosy complexions and happy smiling faces. She was so disappointed and vowed that the first chance she got she would go back home and would never leave her beautiful Ireland again.

Mrs Tate, the woman who had met Bridie, left her at her uncle's front door saying she could not stop because she was in a hurry to get home, then carried on further up the street to where she lived. Her uncle's door was half-open, but Bridie knocked as she was feeling quite nervous and shy. Four small children came running along the passage, shouting "She's here, she's here". A woman with frizzy red hair and lots of freckles on her white face came to the door with a small baby in her arms. The woman who was smiling said, "Come on in Bridie, we have been waiting for you". Bridie liked her straight away and knew this must be her Aunt Shelagh, then followed her and the shouting children along a dark passageway that led into a duller kitchen. Beside the fireplace was a man sitting almost on top of the small fire burning in the hearth. He stood up, went over to Bridie, shook her hand and asked how her mother was. Before Bridie could reply, he turned his back then walked back to his chair covering all of the fire with his long thin legs then he closed his eyes as if he were going to sleep.

Bridie was shocked to the bone. This was not the welcome she had been expecting. She thought she was going to 'well-off' relations as her uncle was always boasting about his great life in England. But looking around her Bridie knew this was not so. Willy was sitting in the only armchair. A wooden table with benches at either side stood in the centre of the floor and an old dresser that was littered with all sorts of things, standing against the wall. The walls had dark green and brown wallpaper torn in places that made the room so dark and miserable. This house was so different to their home in Ireland, where the house was so bright and cheery, with its whitewashed walls and welcoming open turf fare. The picture Bridie had had in her mind of her uncle all these years was entirely different from what he was. He was so tall and thin, must be at least seven-foot tall. She never expected him to have such a big moustache, but what sickened her the most he had a constant drip on his nose so Bridie was pleased he did not give her a kiss and she shivered at the thought of it.

Aunt Shelagh, who was looking very embarrassed, took hold of Bridie's arm saying, "Come upstairs Bridie, I will show you where you will be sleeping". They went up the bare wooden stairs where Bridie followed her aunt into a bedroom that had a double bed, two cots and a small wardrobe with very little room to walk around. It also had the same dark, flowery wallpaper on the walls with patches all over it where the children had torn it and left hanging. Shelagh with the baby resting on her hip, the other children jumping and shouting on the bed said, "Well Bridie I wish I could give you a bedroom of your own, but we only have two bedrooms. I hope you don't mind, but you will have to share the bed with your cousins, the two youngest sleep in the cots". Shelagh who could sense Bridie's disappointment said, "I would like to take one of the cots out and have the baby in our bedroom. It would also give you a little more space in here, but your uncle Willy does not like the children sharing our bedroom". I would like to bet he does not like the children in the house, never mind the bedroom, Bridie thought to herself.

Bridie felt very unhappy. She liked her Aunt Shelagh very much, and she was also sad for all of them because it was not long before she realised that her Uncle was a lazy lout and drunkard. The children loved having Bridie there as she would tell them stories, she would also take them to school then do shopping at the Co-op if there was any money. Then at the weekend, she loved taking all the children to the park to see the swans and baby ducklings. It was also good to get some fresh air away from the grey smoke billowing out of the chimneys.

It was now three weeks since Bridie arrived in England. She realised her uncle had no intention or influence in finding her a job so she told herself that she must go out and find one for herself, even though she would be lucky to find one as many men were out of work. Bridie would get very disheartened when she went around seeing men standing outside the shipyards, men begging for a job to feed their families, hoping it may be their lucky day to be picked for work.

One morning, very early, Bridie crept out of the house and made her way down to 'Paddy's' shipyard just down the road to where they lived. She was the first person at the gates. She stood shivering with the cold as the crowd of men and women got bigger behind her. At 6.30 am a side door opened a man came out and shouted I need two joiners and one woman for the sheds, Bridie's arm shot up in the air. The man said, looking at all the hands up, you, you and pointing to Bridie 'you'. She was walking on air when told to report for work the next day. It was like a dream. Bridie could not believe how lucky she had been; she was so looking forward to starting work.

At last, she would be earning money to send home to her mother. She would also save some of it for her fare back home to Ireland her beloved country. Bridie had written to her mother feeling very guilty that she had no money to send her, so she never said how unhappy she was or anything about her uncle or how badly he treats his family.

The following morning Bridie was up before six o'clock to start her first job. She had very little sleep as she was too excited. She reported to Mr Brown, the foreman, just before seven-thirty. Mr Brown was a small, bald-headed man with a pleasant face, and Bridie felt at ease with him at once. He invited her into his office then offered her a chair to sit on. As this was Bridie's first job, she was quite nervous, but Mr Brown had sensed this. He explained what the job entailed and what she would be doing herself. Before taking her into the shed where she would be working, Mr Brown said, "If you are worried about the job you can always come and see me. I am a good listener. But they are a good bunch of lasses that you will be working with, so I am sure you will not have any problems, but if you have, I am always here." Bridie was introduced to the foreman who took her to the machine where she was to work. She felt very nervous at the loud noise of the machines but put on a brave face pretending not to notice. She met the girls she was to work with, and they soon got down to showing their new workmate the job.

Bridie soon picked up the workings of the job, she also got on very well with all the girls, but she did find the work very tasking, so by the end of the day, she was quite exhausted. Then when she got home, she felt obliged to help her Aunt Shelagh with the children. So, when she eventually went to bed, she fell asleep as soon as her head touched the pillow. The first week at work went very well for Bridie, and now that it was Friday, she would receive her first pay packet. She was loving being at work and being among people of her own age, and they were always laughing and larking about. She became very friendly with Jane Nelson, one of the girls she walked home with. Jane said that she was from Lurgan in Co. Armagh and came to England with her parents when she was a child. Jane invited Bridie to tea at her house on the following Sunday. Bridie was delighted to accept her new friend's offer.

The foreman came around, handing out the wages for that week. Bridie eagerly opened her small brown paper packet to find she had made one pound five shillings. She felt as if she were six feet tall as she waved goodbye to her workmates then headed for home. Bridie went whistling down the street; she had not felt so happy in such a long time. When Bridie went into the house, she took off her coat and overalls then asked her Aunt how much money she wanted off her for her board and lodgings, feeling very grown-up and independent.

Before Shelagh could answer, her Uncle looked up from his paper and said: "Give her a pound". "But Willy", began Shelagh. "Be quiet woman", he snapped, "Do as I say". Bridie was shocked and saddened at having to hand over so much. The girls at work only had to give their mother four or five shillings. She did not say anything but handed over the money to her bewildered Aunt. What hurt Bridie the most was knowing that her Uncle would spend most of it on drink. She would have to ask for overtime as she desperately needed it to send money home to her mother. What would mother think of her sending no money? After all, that is why she had come to England.

On Sunday mornings, Bridie and Shelagh would take the children to mass while her Uncle lay in bed reading the Sunday newspaper. This Sunday, after mass, Jane introduced Bridie to her parents and three brothers Tom, Dan and Sean. The lads were very friendly. They all worked in Swan Hunters shipyard as did their father. Mrs Nelson said in a lovely manner that she would see Bridie at teatime as she had to get home to prepare their Sunday dinner. It was almost four o'clock when Bridie knocked at the Nelson's front door. She got a lovely warm welcome from all the family. Mary and Tommy Nelson were a homely Irish couple just like the folk back home. Mrs Nelson even made some soda bread as a special treat for Bridie. After tea Bridie got to know all the family, she told them all about herself, and for the first time since coming to England, she felt happy and contented. Later in the evening, friends of the family called, some of them bringing a bottle with them, so it ended up them having an Irish party. Everyone was expected to sing a song, but Bridie and Jane were too shy to sing by themselves, so they sang 'Teddy O'Neill' together. It was nearing ten o'clock when Bridie said she would have to go home. Mrs Nelson told Tom to put on his coat and walk Bridie back to her Uncles' house, then she said, "Remember Bridie you are welcome to come here anytime, now goodnight child and god bless you".

Bridie had really enjoyed herself at the Nelson's; it was just like being back home. She wrote to her mother and told her all about it and of all the friends she had made at work, but she never mentioned of how she disliked her Uncle or how cruel he was or about how terribly homesick she felt at times.

The highlight of Bridie's week was when she received a letter from her mother giving her all the news from home, also thanking her for the few shillings she sent. Maggie was always asking Bridie when she would be going back home for a holiday, but Bridie was never able to save enough money to go back, but Bridie never told her why.

Chapter 4

Time went by, and the family back home were all growing up now, Tom was to marry Eileen Casey, an old school friend of Bridies. Also, Danny was about to leave for America, Aunt Rosie, who was well settled in Chicago, had sent his fare saying he would get a job on the police force. Bridie shed a few tears when she read her mother's letter. She was ever so pleased that Tom was about to marry his childhood sweetheart, but she felt sad at the thought of Danny going off to America because it was so far away. She could still picture her young brother with a cheeky grin and a mop of red hair running around in his bare feet trying to catch one of Tommy Connor's chickens, but now he was a young man about to leave home to work. Bridie's family and home were never far from her mind, but she had many good friends in Wallsend, and she thanked God every day for them. They never had a great deal of money, holidays were out of the question, but they knew how to enjoy themselves.

At the weekend's if the weather was fine, a group of them would go down to Whitley Bay, they would take a picnic then spend all day on the beach playing leapfrog, throwing a ball to each other or have a paddle in the North Sea before getting the tram back to Wallsend, tired out and very hungry. If the weather were not so good, they would go to each other's houses. Bridie was always included even though they all knew she could not ask them to her Uncle's house. All the girls looked forward to the Friday night social, this was where Bridie met a lot of Irish people who had settled in Wallsend, so there was always one of them would get up to sing an Irish song. Alcohol was not allowed in the hall, and Father Travers would show his face to make sure they were all keeping on the straight and narrow.

On Thursday nights Father O'Connell, the curate held a social, so on a Wednesday, the girls stayed in to wash their hair. At this social the men and woman would do their own thing, they would all have a cup of tea to start with, then, Father O'Connell would have a chat to them all, adding a few silly jokes. Then the men would usually play cards while the girls played table tennis or sat around chatting. It was at one of these socials that Bridie first met Sean Lavin. Jane the next day shouted to Bridie as she ran to catch up with her friend on their way to work, "I nearly overslept this morning", she said panting for breath. "I enjoyed the social last night, did you?" asked Jane with a big wide grin on her face. "Alright", smiled Bridie, "I can see you are up to something, what's that silly grin on your face for?". "Well," said Jane, "Who was that handsome chap you were talking to? He had the most beautiful blue Irish eyes; he never took them off you all night".

"Oh him", said Bridie walking quite cockily trying not to show how flattered she felt. "That was Sean Lavin, and he comes from my county, we were just talking about places that we both know. I know the area he comes from its only about seven or eight miles from Dunclare. Anyway, I'm not interested, he is too old for me, he must be going on for thirty at least".

"Are we going to the dance tonight?" Jane asked, "Now why wouldn't we, of course, we are, you know I would not miss it for the world. I will call for you at seven o'clock", Bridie told her friend as they both hurried along the road arm in arm to work.

On a Friday, the girls always hurried home to get ready

for the dance. Bridie would iron a blouse to wear also while she had the iron, she would press some clothes for her Aunt. Aunt Shelagh was not in good health, so Bridie helped her whenever she could. There was always a pile of clothes to be ironed; it would take a long time to get through them as they only had one flat iron. The iron was heated on the fire, but it would get cold quite quickly, so you then had to wait until it heated up again.

Every Saturday afternoon, after she came in from work, Bridie helped with the housework. She would be on her knees washing the bare lino floors then she would 'Donkey-stone' the front step, theirs was one of the smartest doorsteps on the street now. Shelagh and Bridie were the best of friends; Bridie felt so sorry for her Aunt as her Uncle treated her so badly. He never lifted a finger to help her even when she was ill. Willie would spend all day Saturday in the pub so when Bridie finished her chores she would sit with Shelagh and tell her all about the dance the previous night.

On this Friday when Bridie had finished the ironing, she took a basin of hot water up to her bedroom to have a good wash before getting ready for the dance. She was ready by seven o'clock, and Shelagh walked to the front door with her, "You look lovely and smart Bridie", said Shelagh. "Have a great time, wish I was going with you", she whispered. Poor Aunt Shelagh thought Bridie as she walked up the street. Her Aunt was still a young woman but never got the chance to go anywhere, her Uncle saw to that.

On one occasion Shelagh asked him if she could go with Bridie to Jane's house, as some of the girls from work were going there for a girls night out, Willie gave his wife one of his evil looks and said, "If you go you will have to take your kids with you. If you think for one minute that I am going to look after them, you are more stupid than I thought you were". Shelagh was so embarrassed in front of Bridie that she never asked him again.

Jane was just putting on her coat when Bridie called for her. The Nelson boys were all bustling about getting ready to go for a drink before going to the dance, all of them laughing and joking with each other. Mr Nelson was sitting in his usual chair by the fireside smoking his pipe and reading the newspaper oblivious to what was going on around him.

Mrs Nelson was busy ironing the white starched collars for the boys. What a lovely atmosphere there always was in their home thought Bridie, such a big difference from the house she had just left. Jane and Bridie said goodbye to all of them, telling the boys that they would see them later at the dance.

The music was already playing when they got to the church hall. It always gave Bridie a warm tingling feeling when she heard the Irish music. The dance was great, Bridie and Jane were up for every dance, both of them loving every minute. The band was called 'The Bryan O'Leary Accordion Band' made up with four local Irish lads who were all talented musicians, they had just started to play for dances.

They got a good reception from them all in Wallsend, and they would certainly be asked back again. It was at these dances young people first met, and romances started not only with Irish couples but also the local boys and girls, so there was a lot of second-generation Irish in the area. The night was almost over, and the last waltz was announced. Dick Conway who had been on a couple of dates with Jane asked her up, then Sean Lavin who had sat all night never up for one dance, asked Bridie if she would like to have a dance. When they were dancing, after chatting for a while, Sean asked Bridie if he could walk her home, Bridie thought why not as he was the best-looking man in the hall. She would make a lot of the girls jealous as she knew most of them fancied him.

When the dance finished, Bridie told Sean she would see him at the door as she had to get her coat from the cloakroom. As they slowly walked along the high street Sean took hold of Bridie's hand, she felt quite shy at first, but she also had a nice, contented feeling. She was pleased that he had asked her instead of one of the other girls. Sean had a nice quiet, but an intelligent way of talking and Bridie was enjoying the conversation.

Sean told Bridie he was one of thirteen children and was the seventh son of a seventh son. Laughing about it, he said that it was supposed to be lucky and that this night he felt lucky, as the best-looking girl in Wallsend had let him walk her home. Then he squeezed her hand in his. He went on to tell Bridie that when he had left home in Boyle, he went to stay with his brother Michael and family in a small mining village in Scotland. He had worked in the coal mine there for five years before coming to Wallsend to start work at The Rising Sun Pit.

When they arrived at Bridie's front door they stood talking for a while, Bridie telling Sean a little about herself, then Sean took Bridie into his arms and kissed her. Bridie felt warm and comfortable in Sean's strong but gentle arms, but she still felt a little shy so said she would have to go in as it was getting late.

Bridie was thinking of her Uncle who had made it quite clear often enough to her that she had to be in by ten-thirty while she was living under his roof if she wasn't the bolt would be put in the door. "Bridie", Sean said, "I know this is our first date together, but I want to tell you I have been in love with you from the first moment I saw you". Then taking hold of Bridie's hands, he said, "Will you marry me Bridie? I will make you a good husband I really will", he said smiling. Bridie tossed her head and laughed as she opened the door, then teasingly she whispered as she went through the door, "I will think about it". Her head was in the clouds, and she felt as if she was walking on air as she walked into the kitchen, but her heart dropped to see that her Uncle was still up. "Put the kettle on and make a cup of tea darlin", he said, smiling at her. "I hope you had a good time at the dance. Was the band good? I bet you had all the young men after you for a dance". Bridie was amazed and wondered why her Uncle was being so nice to her. He had never said very much to her in all the time she was here.

All Bridie wanted to do was go straight to bed as she was very tired, but she went into the scullery and put on the kettle, as she did not want her Uncle to start an argument and wake everyone up. After putting on the kettle, Bridie took off her coat then hung it on a nail behind the cupboard door in the hallway. As she went back through the kitchen to make the tea, her Uncle looked up and said, "Your Aunt has been in bed most of the evening", he was speaking in a whisper, "I don't know what is wrong with that woman. She is always taking to her bed with something or other". He then stood up also walking toward Bridie said, "You are getting to be a fine-looking woman Bridie Donnelly".

Bridie could hardly believe what she was hearing, then all of a sudden, he put his long thin arms around her, his face close to hers, the horrible smell of drink coming from his breath. Anger welled up so much in

Bridie that she slapped his face and kicked him on the shin. Her Uncle moved backwards, cursing her "You red haired bitch, I will make you pay for that, nobody does that to me and gets away with it". He then moved forward again as if to grab her. Bridie stood quite still, looked him straight in the eye and said, "If you ever lay your hand on me again it will be the last thing you will ever do for I swear to God I will kill you, that is a promise".

Willie sat back in his chair then Bridie walked into the scullery turned off the gas under the kettle then went straight up to bed. She undressed, put on her nightie, then knelt down to say her night prayers before climbing into bed trying not to disturb her young cousins. It took Bridie a long time to get to sleep that night as she was shaking, not with fear but for the utter contempt, she felt for her Uncle as he had spoilt one of the happiest nights she had since coming to this country.

The next day Bridie never mentioned the terrible ordeal she had encountered the night before to her Aunt Shelagh as she had enough to worry about without adding more worries for her.

When Bridie called at her friend Jane's house that afternoon, she told her and Mrs Nelson what had happened the night before. Without any hesitation, Mrs Nelson said, "Bridie me darlin, I want you to go back to your Uncle's house this very minute and collect your belongings you are going to stay with us from now on". "But you hardly have enough room for your own family", Bridie protested. "My dear child", Mrs Nelson said in her quiet Irish voice, "Sure you are just like one of our own, we will make room for you don't worry your little head about that, now be off with you. Jane, you go with Bridie to help her, I will have the tea ready when you get back."

Bridie knew her Uncle would still be out at the pub, so she took Jane into the house with her. Shelagh was surprised and pleased to see Jane, and then Bridie told her Aunt that she was going to stay with the Nelson's. Shelagh never asked her why but said that she would miss her very much, she then put her arms around Bridie, making her promise that she would go back and visit her and the children.

Chapter 5

The next few months were the happiest that Bridie had known since coming to England. The Nelson family were very good to her treating her as one of their family. The Nelson's did not have a great lot themselves, but they thought nothing of sharing what they had with others. They were the kindest and most generous people that Bridie had known but then again weren't they 'Irish'? Granny Nelson, as everyone called her, always had a big pan of broth simmering away on the kitchen range, and anyone who called were always welcome to a bowl of it.

Sean, who had been in lodgings for such a long time living a carefree life, felt it was time to settle down with a good wife and raise a family. He knew in his heart that Bridie was the one he wanted. Sean and Bridie were still 'walking out' together, but they were mostly with other friends in a group. The times when they were alone, Sean would keep asking her if she would marry him. He knew she could have her pick of any of the young men, and he was terrified that he would lose her to one of them.

As Bridie had a happy disposition, she was very popular with all her friends, she was always joking and larking about with them, but she also had a serious and caring side to her. A lot of the young men had asked her out on a date, but as she was still 'walking out' with Sean, she felt she could not be untrue to him. Bridie felt in her heart that she was not in love with Sean. She did know that he was a good -living man, he would make a wonderful husband, but Bridie always hoped she would find romance like the time all those years ago back home when she fell in love for the first time with that sixteen-year-old circus boy Michael O'Hara.

Every now and then when her thoughts wandered back home to her younger days in Dunclare. Michael would come into her mind, where was he now? was he married with a family of his own perhaps. But that was a million years ago, and life went on, it was no good daydreaming of what might have been.

Bridie never knew what made her accept Sean's proposal as he walked her home one night from the dance. They had just reached the front door. Sean looked at Bridie in amazement his eyes searching her beautiful face, "Are you codding me?" He said. "Of course, not", said Bridie. "I've said I will marry you Sean, and I will". Sean put his strong arms around Bridie then picked her up and swung her around and around. "Put me down, you ejit" laughed Bridie. "I must go in now. I will see you tomorrow". Sean put his strong but gentle arms around her waist and pulled Bridie towards him kissed her gently on the lips then whispered softly, "You have made me the happiest man in the world, I will love you forever Bridie".

Bridie lay in bed that night wondering if she was doing the right thing, asking herself did she love Sean enough to marry him. The Nelson family had been more than kind to her, but Bridie did not want to impose on their good nature for too long. If she married Sean, it would mean she would never have to go back to live in that dreadful house with her Uncle, so Bridie convinced herself that she was doing the right thing. As Bridie lay thinking, she knew her mother was finding life a lot easier now that the girls were all working and Danny sent her money and clothes regular from America and the thought of a feeling of security and home of her own excited her.

The next day Sean and Bridie told Mr and Mrs Nelson and their family the news that they were to be married. All the Nelson family were delighted and happy for them as they all liked Sean very much. Bridie was like a part of their own family, so they wanted the best for her, and they knew Sean would make her a fine husband. "We will have to have a party to celebrate", Jane said, giving Bridie a big hug then gave Sean a peck on the cheek. After mass, the following day Sean and Bridie went in to see Father Toner, the parish Priest, so a date was made for the wedding to take place on the first Saturday after Christmas. When they left the church, they went to see Mrs Conway, Sean's landlady, and she agreed that they could rent two rooms from her. Everything seemed to be happening so fast, but the first thing Bridie did was to write home to her mother to tell her of their forthcoming marriage. Bridie often mentioned Sean in her letters, so Maggie knew quite a lot about him. Maggie was delighted with her daughters' news. She felt so happy for Bridie as she knew by her letters that Sean was a good living man. She was especially pleased that he was an Irish man and from the same county as them too.

Bridie told her mother all about the arrangements they had made for the wedding, that Jane her best friend was to be her bridesmaid and that Sean's brother Michael was coming down from Scotland to be best man. The most exciting part of the letter which Bridie was deliriously happy to relate to her mother was to tell her that they were to go back home for a holiday in the summer. Bridie knew her mother would be as excited as herself when she heard the news.

When Maggie read her daughters' letter, tears filled her

eyes as she held it to her breast, her precious daughter who was a little more than a child when she left home was coming back again after so long a married woman. To Maggie she would always be her child, a child who had to do so much for her and the family in her young life, she deserved some happiness, and she prayed she would find it with Sean, the man she was about to marry.

Christmas day soon came around, and Sean was invited to spend the full day with Bridie and the Nelson family. The following week Bridie and Jane were kept very busy as every night after work they went to Mrs Conway's house to get the two rooms that the newlywed couple were to rent cleaned and ready for them to move into after the wedding. The bedroom was quite small, with a double bed, a small wardrobe and standing in front of a small marble fireplace was an old chest of drawers. The other room that was to be their living room was slightly larger. It consisted of a table and two dining chairs and a small brown leather settee worn away in places with a tartan rug thrown over it. The canvas on the floor was also worn, with pieces torn out of it, but it all looked clean and shiny after they scrubbed the furniture and floors. They were to use the scullery for cooking and washing clothes.

Bridie was lying in bed on the eve of her wedding, her thoughts wandering back home to her childhood, to her brothers and sisters. It seemed such a long time since she had seen anyone from her past. If only her mother could have been here to see her married. Then the pangs of homesickness gripped her stomach as she buried her tear-stained face into the pillow.

The following morning Bridie and the rest of the Nelson family were up early all bustling about getting ready as the wedding was taking place at nine-thirty. Bridie had a quiet word with Mr and Mrs Nelson to thank them for all their kindness to her. She told them that she would always be grateful to them for making the last few months so happy for her and she gave Mr Nelson a kiss for offering to be at her side to give her away at the church.

Jane and Bridie helped each other to dress, and Bridie looked lovely and smart. Every inch a Bride in her new brown suit and cream blouse, also the hat and gloves she had borrowed from a friend at work that matched her outfit perfectly. Bridie looked again at herself in the mirror thinking sadly "What am I doing, I don't want to get married, I want to go back home to be with my family". Everyone was so happy for her Bridie thought sadly, so she realised, even though she had terrible butterflies in her tummy, she could not back out now it was too late. She would have to go through with the wedding.

The bridal party walked from the Nelson's home up the road to St. Columbas Church. It was a lovely sunny but frosty morning, but at least it was not snowing or raining. Sean was already in church with his brother Michael standing next to him as Bridie walked down the aisle on the arm of Mr Nelson. Sean turned to look at her with a lovely smile on his face; he knew in his heart that he was a very lucky man as he thought how beautiful she looked. Bridie's first thoughts when she looked at Sean was how handsome he looked in his new pin-striped suit and waistcoat with his gold watch and chain setting it all off. It was a lovely ceremony with Father Toner saying the nuptial mass. After it was all over, Father Toner shook their hands and wished them life's happiness.

The newlywed couple left the church to have their photograph taken, then with their friends went back to their new home for the wedding breakfast. Mrs Conway had been more than helpful as she had offered the use of her house for the reception, she also had the table all nicely set and the tea ready for them when they got back. Everyone was enjoying their meal then after three or four speeches had been made, they all toasted the happy couple, then the drinks started to flow, and the singing soon began. The first song was one of Sean's favourites 'The Bonny Banks of Loch Lomond' there were lots of jokes and stories told in between the singing.

It was late evening when the guests began to leave, it had been a long day for everyone, but they all had a great time. Sean's pals wanted a real Irish wedding, so they got what they wanted. Jane and Dick were the last to leave, and the two girls had enjoyed every minute laughing at stupid little things that had been said and done.

"It has been a wonderful day Bridie", said Jane, "I wish you all the happiness in the world. I suppose the next wedding will be mine and Dicks. I hope it goes off as well as yours has".

"I'm sure it will", said Bridie, "I want to thank you, Jane, for everything that you have done for me, you have been a very good friend to me over the years. I don't know what I would have done without you; you have been a real brick". Then Bridie put her arms around her friend and gave her a great big hug.

"Goodnight and God bless", Jane shouted back as she walked hand in hand with Dick down the street, leaving the two newlyweds to start their new life together.

Sean and Bridie were very happy and contented with married life, but at the back of Bridie's mind, she still wasn't sure whether she was in love with Sean or was it just a good feeling of being secure. But she still had no doubts that she had done the right thing by marrying Sean.

Bridie was still working at 'Paddy's', but she would try to get home before Sean to cook dinner and have it already for him when he came home. After dinner, they would sit together on the couch and tell each other any news, mostly about work. Then they were both happy to sit and read until it was time for bed. Friday's, Saturday's and Sunday's were days spent with their friends.

They had been married for only six weeks when Bridie received a message at work from the foreman to say there had been accident at the mine. Bridie went to the cloakroom, grabbed her coat off the peg, then ran, not waiting for permission. She ran towards the mine, her stomach churning. The alarm siren, which could be heard all over Wallsend became louder and louder. Bridie stood with other families who had husbands, sons and brothers trapped below the ground, she blessed herself and said a silent prayer as she watched the brave rescue men go down to free the trapped men. Five hours later, Bridie was still standing there grief-stricken, all she could do was to pray for Sean and all the other miners down there in the bowls of the earth.

Someone shouted, "They're bringing them up". Bridie with the rest of the families moved forward, and then they suddenly stopped when they saw the 'Rescue men' bring out three men on stretchers with blankets covering their faces and a group of miners, their faces black with the coal dust, walking slowly behind. Bridie's eyes searched among them for her Sean, tears blurring her vision. 'Was that her name being called?' With all the crying and noise, she may have misheard. Then she heard it again; it was Sean shouting. "Sean, oh Sean", cried Bridie as she ran towards her husband with her arms outstretched. "Oh Sean, thank God you are alright. I couldn't go on living if anything had happened to you. I love you so much". Then Sean took Bridie into his strong arms; there was no need for any more words.

Sean was a strong and healthy man, so he was back at work the following day with some of his 'Marras' (Workmates) to help clear the fall of coal that had sadly killed three of the miners. Holidays were the only time when Sean was off work, he seldom had a cold or illness of any sort, and he never thought of taking a day off as money was in short supply. The miners worked in terrible conditions for very little money. They were made to feel that they were lucky to have a job as there was so much unemployment. They went to work even if they were unfit, as there was always someone to step into their place.

Chapter 6

Spring was now almost over, so Sean and Bridie were looking forward to their holiday in the summer. It was hard for Bridie to believe that at last, she was going back home to Ireland, she was counting the weeks with great excitement. The last couple of weeks, Bridie had been feeling sickly when she got up in the morning, so she went along to see Dr McKenzie. He confirmed her suspicions that she was to have a child. Sean was as happy as Bridie when he heard he was to become a father, to make their family complete. As it was only three weeks before they were to go on their holiday, Bridie assured Sean that she would be well enough to travel and not to fuss as she felt great apart from the morning sickness. The doctor said it would only last a few weeks anyway.

Well, the big day came, and they were on their way back home. Sean was almost as excited as Bridie about going as he wanted to show off his lovely wife to his family and friends. He was also longing to see his mother again as he had not been home for such a long time. They travelled by train to Holyhead where they caught the early morning boat to Dun Laoghaire. Seeing the big ship brought floods of sad memories flooding back for Bridie but she had Sean by her side to look after her now. Bridie's thoughts travelled back to the lady who had befriended her, what was her name again, then it came to her it was Eileen Carey. She remembered how kind she was to her during her sad journey to England. Then she thought of her heartache at leaving her beloved mother. But that was all in the past. She was happy as a lark now with Sean, her handsome husband whom she loved with all her heart and wasn't she going back now to see her mother. Then her heart filled with love and excitement; she could not explain to anyone the wonderful feeling that she felt inside, even if she lived to be a hundred. It was a lovely calm crossing, and the time went quickly. A child looking through a porthole shouted to his mother, "I can see the land."

"Let's go upstairs Sean", said Bridie. Excitedly Sean took hold of Bridie's hand as they made their way upstairs to watch the beautiful shores of Ireland come into view. Bridie's heart was aglow with a feeling of contentment, knowing she was back in her own country. They stayed on deck until the boat docked. Bridie felt dizzy with happiness when she stepped onto her native soil. They did not dawdle about but headed straight for the bus that would take them home. As the bus rolled its way along the winding country lanes, Bridie's eyes searched the beautiful landscape. What a wonderful sight to see the thatched cottages with smoke coming from their chimneys and the comforting smell of the turf fires burning. This is Ireland Bridie thought, with a lovely warm feeling knowing she was back home again in Ireland the land she would always love.

As the bus was nearing Dunclare village Bridie was eager to point out to Sean all the familiar places she knew so well. The police barracks in Elphin where she was born; the ruins of the old castle where she often went to as a child to play with her friends; and the crossroads where she danced on many an occasion. Bridie's excitement calmed down when she realised that she was almost back at home with her mother as Sean stood up and reached for their suitcase that was in the luggage rack above.

The bus came to a halt in Dunclare village, Sean and

Bridie said goodbye to the driver as they stepped off the bus, Bridie's eyes going straight toward the house that had been in her thoughts for so long and standing looking over the half-door was her dear mother. Maggie opened the door walked slowly toward them, then Bridie and her mother hugged each other both of them crying with tears of happiness falling down their cheeks. Sean walked slowly toward the house, leaving Bridie to walk back arm in arm with her mother. Before they knew it, they were surrounded by the rest of the family who had been eagerly awaiting them, all of them trying to talk to Bridie at the same time. When they had calmed down, Bridie introduced Sean to her family. Tom shook Sean's hand and told him he was welcome. Then the girls started making remarks about Sean's handsome good looks saying perhaps they too should go to England if there were any more like him there. Sean was feeling embarrassed by it all, but Bridie felt very proud of her husband. She was also amazed at her sisters, they were now lovely young women, and her brother Tom was a fine-looking man and Eileen her best friend, and now Tom's wife was also lovely.

Bridie was pleased to see her mother looked the picture of health. She has lost that tired look that Bridie remembered of her in her mind but thanked God her mother's life was now less stressful not like days gone by. Bridie's eyes wandered around the kitchen; it was just as she had left it, the big open fire was a sight she had longed to see for so long. The same sacred heart picture hanging over the fireplace and was that the same old besom standing under the stairs she wondered. Also, the friendly black kettle hanging on the crook over the burning sods of turf the steam starting to spout out ready to make tea. The table was still by the window all set for their tea with brown and white soda bread, tomatoes, a big pat of butter and a large jar of strawberry jam. Simple fare by most standards but to Bridie, it looked like a feast. Maggie beckoned everyone to sit down as she placed on the table a plateful of home-cooked ham.

"Things have certainly changed Ma ma", Bridie said, looking lovingly at her mother.

They all chatted during tea, the girls wanting to know everything and anything from Bridie but were very polite and friendly toward Sean. Maggie took a great liking to Sean, her son-in-law, she knew that Bridie had chosen well. He told Maggie all about himself, he told her about his family, that his mother would be eighty come her next birthday, that his father had been a farmer but had died ten years ago. Sean found it easy talking to Maggie. He spoke of Boyle, where he was born and reared.

"I'm sure you must be dying to see your mother Sean", Maggie said. "Sure, I am, it's a long time since I was home, I worry about her as she is not in the best of health, but I know she is well -looked after. I have a brother, and he and his family live with her"

Bridie overheard Sean talking about his mother, and she felt quite guilty and selfish being here with her family around her. When tea was over Sean and Bridie went outside to stand at the front door just looking around the village, Bridie suggested to Sean that he go on ahead tomorrow to his mother's then she would follow him in a few days. Sean was so pleased that Bridie had suggested this to him as he would never have done so himself. He was quite happy being among Bridie's family, they had made him more than welcome, but he was also anxious to get home to see his mother.

Maggie had a kettle of warm water for Bridie to freshen up. Bridie took the basin of water upstairs into the bedroom she used to share with her sisters, she looked around it was almost the same as she left it. The bare wooden floorboards, the same double bed, also the cupboard where they hung their few clothes. Bridie walked over to the small window in the far corner of the room, looked out onto the lovely green fields behind the house, where she had played many a time. She pulled back the pretty lace curtain to have a better look, and she did not know whether to laugh because she was so happy to be back home or to cry, remembering the sad times. Looking around her Bridie had pictured this bedroom in her thoughts many times thinking of when they were young and how on a rainy day, they would spend hours jumping on the bed and having pillow fights. Then the sound of laughter brought her out of her daydream.

Bridie quickly bathed then changed into a nice fresh white blouse, and black skirt then went downstairs to find all the family sitting around the fire all of them wanting to make room for her to sit down beside them. Everyone was asking her questions about her work and where she lived, but Bridie only wanted to hear all about home. How was Mr Ryan over the road? Did his son Bruddy take over the shop? How was Ann Kelly? Barbara Healy? Geraldine Donnelly? and Jane Casey, her dearest school friend? Did they ever see any of them?

"Now Bridie", said Maggie, "We want to hear all about you and Sean. You have not mentioned your Uncle Willy, how are they all keeping?"

Bridie told her mother she had not seen her Uncle for some time, but she was sure he was fit and well, although Aunt Shelagh was not very strong, and she was ill quite often. Then she gave all the news about how their work was going, about where they lived and of all the good friends they had.

Then Bridie smiling turned to look at Sean, saying, "We have a surprise for you". Then quite shyly said, "We are going to have a baby at the turn of the year". The whole family were excited at Bridie's good news, asking if they wanted a boy or girl. Tom was making a joke of it saying they had beaten himself and Eileen to it. Maggie was delighted that she was to become a grandmother. She put her arms around her daughter and gave her a big hug saying, "I know you will make a wonderful mother Bridie. May sweet Jesus and his blessed mother take care of you. I am delighted for you both; this is one of the happiest days of my life. I only wish our Danny could be here with us all to celebrate the good news."

Tom who was always there to cheer his mother up if she was feeling down said, "Sure our Dan is having a great time in America, he got what he always wanted, to be a policeman like Da da. He has plenty of good friends in the force, sure isn't the New York and Chicago police force all Irish anyhow I'm sure it won't be long before he is getting married himself to that Colleen from Co. Donegal that he is always telling us about in his letters.".

Tom stood up then turning to Eileen said, "Well me darlin we better get going we have the cows to milk remember". Then kissing his mother said, "We will be back in a couple of hours, I will pass the word around that Bridie is home so we will have a hooley tonight to celebrate."

Bridie went to the door to see them off. What a lovely

couple they make she thought as she watched them walk up the road. Tom meant a lot to Bridie as he had always been so good to their mother; she was happy too that he had courted and married Eileen. He above all deserved a good happy life as he was the one who worked from a young age to feed the family. Eileen's family had a farm, and the father had built a new house and gave Tom and Eileen their old one. Tom had bought a few cows and chickens, but it was Eileen, a farmer's daughter, who knew how to look after them while Tom still worked as the local postman, but he helped Eileen in his spare time.

When Tom and Eileen had left, Maggie said she would just slip up to see Mrs Moffatt as she had just received the last sacraments but said she would be back shortly. Sean went upstairs to shave and change his shirt, so Bridie was pleased to have a little time to talk to her sisters. Geraldine and Kathleen were both training to be nurses and were living in Dublin. Margaret, the youngest was training to be a hairdresser, Margaret would like to get a job near home. They all had a good chat then Tom and Eileen returned, and before long the house was full as the Ramblers came bringing their tin whistles and fiddles, so the home was alive with music and laughter. Sean and Bridie were enjoying every minute; they danced and sang until the early hours of the morning. It finished as usual with a few yarns which of course delighted them listening to them all after being away from home for so long.

The next morning was Sunday, even though they had little sleep, they were all up early for Mass. Bridie was awake at seven o'clock, and she got straight out of bed, she wanted to enjoy every minute that she would have at home also there was nowhere else on earth more beautiful as Ireland on a lovely summers morning.

Bridie went downstairs to find that her mother was already up sitting on a stool tying up her long silver hair into a bun on the back of her head.

"What a beautiful morning Ma ma," said Bridie.

"It certainly is but you being back here makes it that much nicer", said Maggie, as she opened the top half of the door to let in the bright morning sunshine. "We will have a walk to the well for some freshwater", Maggie said to her daughter as she picked up the white enamel pail from under the table. Bridie put her arm into her mother's as they strolled contentedly toward the well opposite Paddy Degnan's cottage, both of them enjoying these few precious moments they were sharing. When they got back to the house, they found Sean and the girls bustling about getting ready to go to mass. At twenty to nine, Maggie said, "Come along everyone. We will have to go", then she ushered them all out of the house. They had ample time as it only took a couple of minutes to walk to the church, and mass was at nine o'clock, but Maggie would never be last, as she always said the rosary before Mass. Bridie would always remember the happiness she felt that morning as she walked hand in hand with Sean, her dear mother on her other side, as they walked to mass together. The church was soon full to capacity, with an overflow of men standing at the back and even outside in the churchyard. Bridie looked around for familiar faces; she recognised most of them except some of the younger ones. The priest Father Cass was new to her as Father Lynch was now in a parish near Ballina. After mass Bridie was happy to talk to old friends and neighbours, she was also proud to introduce them to Sean. Then all the family, including Tom and Eileen went back home for breakfast.

"I can't get rid of these two", said Maggie laughing, "Tom comes to see his old mother every day don't you son".

"You will be seeing more of me when I get the house next door", Tom replied

"What's all this about then?". said Bridie

"Well now", said Maggie, "Old Mrs O'Neill is almost a hundred years old, I'm sure, so her oldest son Paul wants her to go and live with him and his wife in Castlerea. He has told Tom he can buy her house when they have converted their own home, to accommodate the old lady".

"It will be better for all of us when I get it", said Tom, "I will be nearer the post office. I can move the cattle to the Druid field, and there is plenty of room at the back of the house for the hens. That house of ours needs an awful lot of work done to it. You know yourself what it's like up there in the winter, you could be snowed in for days.

Tom and Eileen left soon after breakfast. Then Sean and Bridie went out for a stroll calling into one or two cottages to say hello to some of the old folk. Bridie would not have been happy if she had not seen everyone.

After dinner, Bridie walked with Sean up to the crossroads to meet Brendon Kelly, who was to give him a ride to French Park. This was to be their first time apart since they were married, and they both sensed each other's lonely feelings. Sean put his strong suntanned arms around his young wife and gave her a lingering kiss. They clung to each other as though it was to be their last. Sean whispered softly in Bridie's ear, "I love you Bridie, I am going to miss you, take care of yourself and that baby of ours".

"I love you too Sean, I am going to miss you, but it will only be for a few days"

Brendon was there right on time with his horse and trap. Then they were off waving goodbye to the tearful Bridie.

The next few days went flying by, but Bridie was savouring every moment of her visit home. She spent a lovely day out with Eileen and her sisters in Derrytagh the small market town. Bridie bought a pretty lace-edged tablecloth to give to Mrs Gough when she called to see her in Elphin. Mrs Gough was delighted when she saw her visitor, and she was so pleased that Bridie had not forgotten her she could not thank her enough for the beautiful gift. She told Bridie that her husband was still the sergeant at the barracks, but she was eager to find out about Bridie and her life in England. Bridie told her about the sad journey she had had when she left home but how she had found happiness with the good friends she had made and of Sean, her wonderful husband.

Thursday soon came around then Bridie was on her way to French Park to see Sean and meet his family. When the bus got to the small town, Sean was there waiting for her in a jaunting car. He jumped down and came towards Bridie with a smile on his face that would melt any woman's heart. They drove the short journey at a nice easy trotting pace to the Lavin's home. Bridie was feeling nervous about meeting Sean's mother for the first time she blathered on about what she had been doing the last few days. Sean knowing how she felt said, "My mother is dying to meet you, I know you will like each other. That is our place just up ahead", Sean said as they turned off the road into a narrow lane.

As they got nearer Bridie's breath was taken away at the sight of their lovely cottage and garden, it was just like a picture postcard. Maria, Sean's mother, came out to greet them. Bridie was surprised at how small she was as Sean was almost six foot. Maria gave her a warm welcome. Bridie could see where Sean had got his lovely blue eyes from. Eamonn, Sean's brother still lived at home with his wife Jane and their four children, Rosie, Claire, Paul and Joe. They were a lovely family and made her feel at home right away. Sean and Bridie were invited to lots of parties, and Sean, of course, was so proud showing off his lovely wife.

Their last night at French Park was spent at home with the family having a quiet drink and talking mostly about old times. They were listening to Maria telling Bridie about Sean when he was a young lad when suddenly two young men looking in a distressed state came rushing into the house. Bridie got a shock at first, but she soon realised who they were, they were boys in the I.R.B 'Irish Republican Brotherhood'.

"The Tans are after us". one of them said. Without anyone saying another word, they were helped up into a loft. Then the family sat around the fire, talking as though nothing had happened. A few minutes later, a group of British Black and Tan soldiers burst into the house. Bridie was quite frightened at the sight of them with their rifles aimed at them. Sean made a move toward Bridie when one of the soldiers aimed his gun at him, saying, "Make a move, and you are a dead man". The soldiers searched the house knocking over furniture as they looked but had to leave without finding the unexpected guests.

Bridie enjoyed her stay at Sean's with his mother; she

found the family very homely, just like her own family. But now they were going back to Dunclare to spend the rest of their holiday. Sean's mother bade them goodbye, as she hugged Bridie, she said to her, "I am happy now that Sean has settled down with a lovely girl like yourself. If the good lord above, takes me tomorrow I will be happy to go now that I have seen all my family settled down". As Sean kissed his mother goodbye, Bridie wiped away a tear as Maria was such a frail dear old lady this may be the last time, they would see each other.

The journey back to Dunclare was quite sad for Sean and Bridie, but they soon cheered up when they arrived there. Over the next few days, Bridie savoured the time she had at home with her mother until it was time to leave.

It was another lovely sunny morning. Bridie was up bright and early. Tom called and had breakfast with them before he went off to work as this was the morning they were going back to England. But she still wished with all her heart that she could stay here forever.

The bus arrived in the village near lunchtime, the bus that would take them on the start of their long journey back to Wallsend. It was another tearful goodbye with Sean and Bridie promising them all that they would be back next year please God bringing with them their new baby. Margaret, Bridie's youngest sister, making them promise they would name the baby after her if it was a girl. Bridie hugged her mother, why did it have to be so painful saying goodbye to the ones you love, most of all to mothers because that bond could never be broken. Did it have to be so painful saying goodbye to the ones you love, Bridie's heart cried. It also brought back painful memories of when she first left home. This time she should not be feeling so sad for did not she have Sean her husband a man she loved with all her heart, a man she was building a new life with. But she was still desperately sad at leaving her mother. She knew too, that part of her heart would always be here.

Chapter 7

Sean and Bridie soon settled down again when they returned to Wallsend after their wonderful holiday back home. They went back to work and into their usual routine of everyday life also looking forward to the birth of their baby due in the new year. Sean was well respected at the colliery as he was a good worker and never lost a day's work. So, when he asked the manager to be considered for a colliery house even though he had no family, yet he was pleasantly surprised when they gave him keys for a three-bedroomed house. He knew Bridie would be elated.

That evening when they had finished dinner Sean said to his young wife, "I think we will go out for a stroll tonight".

"What?" said Bridie "In the middle of the week? I thought we were going to have a few early nights for a change. I don't know about you Sean, but I still have not got over all those late nights we had over home".

"Well me darlin I have a big surprise for you. Sean put his hand into his waistcoat pocket and brought out two keys. These are for number 42 Laurel Crescent; it's ours if we want it."

"I can't believe it, Sean, how did you get it?" Bridie asked in utter amazement

"Never mind about that me darlin, get your coat on and let's be away to have a look at it", Sean said smiling.

The house was in the street where the Nelsons lived. Bridie could hardly believe how lucky they were to get a place so quickly and in the same street where their best friends lived. Laurel Crescent consisted of terraced houses. The colliery owned one side of the street, providing housing for the miners and the other side was owned by the shipyard for their workers. The street was not that big, so everyone knew each other; everyone was quite friendly wherever they worked.

Sean opened the front door and went in first, not knowing what to expect, but they were pleased to find it nice and clean even though the paintwork was either brown or green. The small hallway led into the main room; it had a lovely coal fire with a black range with an oven and a brass fender around it. The house had a lovely warm and cosy feeling to it. In the scullery, there was a sink, a small wooden bench, a small gas cooker and in the corner was a boiler for the clothes. Off the scullery was the stairs leading to three bedrooms. They both looked all around the house then went into the backyard that had the toilet and coal house.

"Well what do you think of it?" asked Sean

"Oh, I love it Sean", said Bridie, giving her husband a kiss. "All it needs is a few coats of paint to brighten it up. We can emulsion the walls in a nice colour".

"You can have it what way you want darlin", said Sean, so pleased that Bridie liked the house.

Still, very excited, Bridie said, "We will come back tomorrow to measure up for curtains, Jane will be in her element sewing them. Did you know she has just bought an old singer sewing machine?"

"Great", said Sean, pretending to be interested. "We won't have any rent to pay, and we will get a free load of coal every month so we will have extra money to spend on the house. But I will leave those sort of things to you as I am no good at things like that"

The free rent and coal were supposed to be a perk for the miners. But they worked in terrible conditions in the bowels of the earth for a mere pittance, so the free rent and coal was designed to appease the workforce. When Sean and Bridie came out of their new home, they headed straight across the road to tell their friends the Nelson's the good news. Jane said she would go with Bridie to choose her curtains and that she would be delighted to sew them. The Nelson lads said they would help Sean to paint the house also if they needed any joinery work done, they would do it. They could always get what they needed from the shipyard, so it would not cost them a penny.

Within a fortnight Sean and Bridie moved into their new home. As they had no furniture, they just bought the bare necessities, friends had also bought housewarming gifts, so they had plenty to get by on. They bought, lovely flowered patterned canvas for the floors, one of their friends had made them a colourful Clippy mat to go in front of the fireplace. Everything looked lovely after they had polished it all and ornaments, they had received as wedding presents set the place off. It all looked so nice and cosy when Jane put up the curtains. She had also made some cushion covers to match as a housewarming gift. The house was blessed by Father Toner when they moved in. Then on the following Saturday, they held a party for their friends. All the Nelsons came, also Martin and Bea Casey, Wilf Rice and a host of their friends, so they had a real Irish party with plenty of singing. Bridie felt so contented in her new home, the home that Sean and herself would spend all their married life.

Soon after they moved in Bridie invited her Aunt

Shelagh and the children for tea, it was on a Saturday as she knew her Uncle would be in the pub all day. She baked some soda bread, stotty cake, rhubarb tart, fruit scones and fairy cakes. The tea table was all set out looking very appetising, when they came, Sean and Bridie both greeted them at the door, welcoming them all in.

Shelagh's eyes lit up as she looked around her, "Oh Bridie your home is lovely. It's so bright and clean, I hope you both will be very happy here, but I know you will".

Bridie knew Shelagh meant every word she said as she did not have a jealous bone in her body. They all had a lovely day, Shelagh enjoying the laughter and the Irish humour, something she never had in her own home. Sean played with the children then walked them back carrying the young one on his shoulders.

Christmas Eve was Bridie's last day at work. At lunchtime, her friends who she worked with all wished her well as they gave her gifts for the new baby. They all said she would be greatly missed. Mrs Nelson invited Sean and Bridie to spend Christmas day with them, but Bridie knew she had her own big family to cook for. It would also be nice for Sean and herself to spend their first Christmas as man and wife together in their new home, but they promised that they would go over at teatime to spend a couple of hours with them.

All the festive holidays were over now, so Bridie was getting prepared and excited about the birth of her first baby due in a few weeks. Tommy Nelson had made a lovely wooden cradle 'in his spare time' down in the shipyard. Bridie made a mattress and pillow for it then she went shopping with Jane to buy the necessary clothes that the baby would need.

It was early in the morning on January 29th that Bridie was having niggly pains and she realised that her labour had begun. She crept out of bed not wanting to wake Sean, but by six o'clock, she had to ask him to go and get the midwife Nurse Thompson as her pains were getting very strong. Nurse Thompson, the local midwife, was well known in Wallsend, she always went around on her bicycle with her black bag. The local children always thought she brought a new baby in the bag. The midwife examined Bridie then went downstairs to ask Sean if he could get a friend or neighbour that could come in just in case there could be any complications.

"So, you think there could be?", asked Sean looking very worried and white-faced.

"Of course, not", laughed Nurse Thompson, "It is just precaution, I'm sure everything will be fine. Make yourself a cup of tea there's nothing to worry about".

Before making the tea, Sean ran across the road for Mrs Nelson, who left what she was doing to go with Sean. By ten o'clock that morning, Bridie gave birth to a beautiful baby daughter. Sean was sitting by the fireplace when he heard the nurse and Mrs Nelson talking as they came down the stairs. He stood up as they came in, Nurse Thompson smiled at Sean saying, "Well Mr Lavin, you have a beautiful, healthy daughter 7lb. 6oz". Sean's face lit up then shook her hand and thanked her. He kissed Mrs Nelson then ran up the stairs two at a time. Sean crept slowly into the bedroom to see his wife and new-born child. The baby was wrapped in a fluffy white towel and was lying in Bridie's arms. Sean was the happiest man in the world as he kissed his wife then the baby.

"I'm sure she has your nose", laughed Bridie as she

gently touched the soft cheek of their baby

"God forbid", smiled Sean, "I'm sure she is as beautiful as her mother".

After a week in bed, Bridie was up taking care of her baby and husband, and busy making arrangements for the christening in a few days. Of course, Jane was delighted and honoured when asked to be godmother to the baby who was to be named Margaret after Bridie's youngest sister.

Chapter 8

Over the next few years, Bridie was quite content being a wife and mother, and her family were her life as she had four more children Catherine, James, Mary and Patrick. Sean and Bridie were excellent parents; people would comment on what a lovely close family they were. But money was short now that there was only Sean's wage coming in. They managed as best they could, but it was quite difficult for them at times.

Conditions at the mines were getting worse. The wages were so low, and the miners felt the greedy owners were exploiting them. So a general strike was called. Most homes had little or no money coming in, Sean with other miners would go to the pit head late at night to gather coal that was lying around to sell for a few pennies. Eventually, men all over the country returned to work without gaining anything. It was a case of, go back to work or let their families starve with hunger.

 Friday was always payday the best day of the week. Wives were always waiting for their husbands to come home with their wages, and children would always get a 'pay-penny' off their daddy to buy sweets. The first thing Bridie bought was flour and yeast to bake the bread for her family, so their home was always warm with the lovely smell of fresh bread cooking. Neighbours would borrow a few pence off each other until payday, but Bridie always prided herself that she never had to borrow but often lent the woman next door two and six ', but she always paid it back'.

Every Thursday night Bridie always had a couple of pennies left which she kept on purpose for the children.

She would say to them "I have two pennies left; I wonder what I should do. Shall I keep them for the gas meter in case the light goes out or shall we get two pennyworths of chips". There would always be a chorus of voices shouting, "Chips, chips". Margaret would run up to Metcalfe's fish and chip shop at the top of their street to get a big bag of chips with lots of lovely crunchy batter. The chips would be shared out, and Bridie would give them a big piece of stottie cake with butter on, then they would all sit around the fire just as Bridie had done with her mother. Then she would tell them the stories that she had heard when she was young. The family would always ask for a ghost story, so Bridie always made a one up for them.

The story always ended by someone in the story getting their leg pulled so Bridie would say to them, "The same way that I am pulling yours".

The children would all shout that it was not fair.

The family all loved their mother telling them about when she was young and all the true tales, she would tell them. Sean would be sitting in his chair, reading a book and smoking his pipe. He would look up now and then to smile at Bridie as she had their constant attention, not one of them taking their eyes off their mother totally engrossed in the stories she was telling them.

Most of Sean and Bridie's friends were all settled down with families of their own, so they did not see as much of each other as they used to. But they would see most of them at mass on a Sunday, and they all tried to get to the dance on the last Friday of each month where they would catch up with all the news. Shelagh, Bridie's aunt, sadly passed away with consumption her family who were all grown up by now still called to see Bridie and confide in her like a mother.

Sadly, Jane and her husband were childless, herself and Bridie were still the best of friends. Jane called in most days to see the children and give Bridie a helping hand if she needed it, she was always there for her friend.

Bridie's youngest sister Margaret wrote to say that she was coming to Wallsend for a holiday. She was now a qualified hairdresser. She was also engaged to be married to Paul Heaney, a young man in the Irish Army. Margaret said she would tell Bridie all about her handsome sweetheart and of her plans for their wedding next spring. Bridie was overjoyed that her sister was coming; it was such a long time since she had seen any of her family. The children were very excited too, telling their friends about their aunt coming all the way from Ireland.

Jane went with Bridie up to Newcastle Central Station to meet Margaret. They were there long before her train was due in as Bridie never forgot the day that she arrived in Newcastle to find that no one was there to meet her and how frightened and lonely she felt. Bridie was pleased that Margaret would see her and Sean's lovely home. Also, she was longing to show off her beautiful children so she could tell their mother all about them when she went back to Dunclare.

Jane stood with her excited friend outside the ticket barrier at No.2 platform when the passengers started to come through.

"There she is", cried Bridie, as she ran toward her sister waving her hand. Margaret put down her suitcase then they threw their arms around each other. She was so beautiful thought Bridie. The suit she was wearing was so smart, and she felt very proud that this was her sister. She introduced Margaret to her friend Jane, and they shook hands, then Margaret with a beautiful smile said,

"I feel I know you already Jane as Bridie is always talking about you in her letters home".

"Not bad things I hope", laughed Jane.

"No, not at all, Jane", Margaret said, still smiling. "She tells us how the two of you are such good friends, so I hope you will be mine too while I am here".

"Here, give me your suitcase. I will carry it for you. That's a good start now isn't it" laughed Jane.

They all laughed about it then Bridie put her arm into Margaret's as they all walked out of the dull dark railway station into the lovely bright sunshine. Bridie looked at her sister and said, "I can't wait to hear all the news, Margaret. But first, tell me how is ma ma?"

"Oh, she is in fine fettle", smiled Margaret with a smile lighting up her lovely young face. "She sends all her love. I have some soda bread and butter in my bag that she has sent you".

Jane suggested that they go for a cup of tea before catching their train for Wallsend. The suitcase was starting to feel quite heavy. They crossed over the road then Margaret stopped and looked around her.

"What's the matter hen?" said Bridie, as she saw a puzzled look on her sister's face.

"I know this may sound ridiculous, but I have this strange feeling that I have been here before", Margaret said, then looking at Bridie and Jane said, "I am sure if we go around the next corner there is a café about three doors up".

None of them spoke another word but walked along the street then around the corner sure enough there it was just as Margaret described it.

"Oh, it's just a coincidence", Bridie laughed, trying to make a joke of it, but inside her heart gave a flutter of unease, then she said a silent prayer.

When they got home to Wallsend Mrs Nelson, who had been looking after the family had the tea ready for them, then after being introduced to Margaret left saying she would be seeing them later. The older children were already in from school all sitting quietly not taking their eyes off their lovely young aunt, all the way from Ireland. It did not take long for everyone to be at ease, Margaret had a lovely bubbly bright personality you could see that she and the children would be the best of friends. After Bridie had shown Margaret around the house, Margaret told her sister that she should be very proud of her home and family. Bridie was already very proud of her family, but it was nice of her sister to say so. Sean would be home from work soon, so Margaret helped her sister fill the long tin bath with hot water for him to bathe in front of the fire.

"Hello Margaret", Sean said, smiling, his teeth looking very white against the black coal dust on his face. "How are you? Welcome to Wallsend, I hope you enjoy your stay with us", giving her a little peck on the cheek.

Bridie left towels on the floor beside the bath then ushered Margaret and the children into the scullery saying, "Come away with you all while Daddy has his bath, I am sure he doesn't want an audience".

While they were waiting for Sean to have his bath Bridie was seeing to Sean's dinner as she liked to have it on the table when he was finished. Sean had two meals every day. He would have bacon and eggs for breakfast, and for dinner, he always had lots of potatoes and meat with cabbage. He would only take a couple of slices of bread and jam to work.

After everything was cleared away and they had time to talk and relax, Margaret gave Bridie all the news from home. She told them all about Paul, her fiancé that he came from Co. Mayo and that he was in the Irish Army, but they were hoping to go to Chicago where their brother Danny was. Danny loved the police force and said Paul would get on the force without any problem Margaret said full of confidence while she bounced baby Patrick on her knee.

"We are thinking of having a spring wedding next year. I would love it if you could all come for it".

"I would love to Margaret," Bridie said, feeling quite excited. "But we will have to wait and see, God's good, you never know what might turn up."

Margaret soon made herself at home, she was really enjoying her holiday and being with her sister and her lovely family. She loved going to the big shops in Newcastle. She had never been in such big shops before. She bought herself a lovely dress, also a nice blouse for her mother and one for Bridie. She liked Bridie's friends when she met them at the dance on the Friday night. Jane and Bridie were laughing about them being wallflowers as it was Margaret who was getting to dance with all the men. Even though Margaret was being asked for dates, she refused, as she was true to her sweetheart Paul.

Margaret was a happy go lucky girl always full of devilment; all the children loved her as she was such good fun. The family would go down to the beach, and Margaret would play for hours with the children. They would paddle in the sea, build sandcastles or play with the bat and ball then she would buy them ice cream. When they got back home, they would have their tea, then the young ones were ready for bed all tired out by the sea air and running around on the beach.

As Margaret was a qualified hairdresser, she cut and styled Bridie's hair for her. When Jane saw how nice it was, she asked Margaret to do hers too. When Jane's hair was done, Bridie said to Margaret that she had come in useful, so would she come back again when they needed their hair cut. Margaret, who enjoyed their humour, said, "Yes, of course, I will, just pick up the phone and make an appointment".

"What's a phone?" they both laughed.

The holiday for Margaret was almost over she would soon be heading back home to Ireland. The children were all feeling sad as they loved their aunt and wished she could stay with them forever. On Thursday morning two days before Margaret was due to leave Bridie told Sean that their youngest daughter Mary and her sister were too ill to get out of bed.

"I am worried about them, Sean, will you go for the doctor".

Dr McKenzie came before his morning surgery. Bridie took him straight upstairs explaining as they went up that Margaret was here on holiday but was going home in two days' time. The doctor examined Mary first then Margaret; he never spoke until they were back downstairs.

"Mrs Lavin," he said. "They both have pneumonia, and I am quite concerned about your sister, she is very ill. I think you should inform your mother."

Mrs Casey, a friend of the family who was talking to Sean, said she would go to the post office and send the telegram for them. Mrs Nelson and Jane offered to care for the children as Sean had to go to work while Bridie kept a vigil at the bedside of her daughter and sister. Dr McKenzie had left medicine for them, but he came back after his evening surgery, he said there was little change but said he would call again in the morning. Bridie was praying that by tomorrow they would both be well again; Margaret could always get another boat in a few days. A telegram arrived from Maggie Bridie's mother saying she would be over the next day. The following morning the doctor called very early, he told Bridie that he was still concerned about them both adding that Margaret had not responded at all to the medicine.

"I will call back later tonight to see them. Keep giving them their medication".

Sean went up to Newcastle to meet Maggie off the boat train. When he saw her, his heart went out to his mother-in-law as she looked very pale and tired looking. Sean took her small case then put his arm through hers as they went for the tram. Bridie broke down and cried as she hugged her beloved mother as she looked so ill herself. Maggie was not a young woman anymore; she was exhausted by the long journey, also the worry of her youngest daughter on her mind. Maggie had to be coaxed away from Margaret's bedside to have something to eat and drink. Maggie told them that Paul, Margaret's fiancé, was to get compassionate leave from the army and that he would be here in a couple of days. That evening when the doctor called, he gave Maggie a sedative to take, he said she needed to have a good night's sleep.

On the third morning after Maggie arrives, Dr McKenzie called as usual before his morning surgery. Bridie followed him into Mary's bedroom, after examining her he said she was over the critical stage and that she should be fine in a week or two.

"Oh, thank God, thank God", said Bridie, looking down at her young daughter who was asking for a drink.

Bridie then followed the doctor into Margaret's bedroom. She knew straight away by the way the doctor looked that all was not well. Dr McKenzie took hold of Bridie's arm, beckoning her to leave the bedroom, they went downstairs and into the kitchen before he spoke.

"I am very sorry, Mrs Lavin, but I cannot do anymore for your sister".

"What do you mean doctor? Is Margaret going to die?"

"I am very sorry, we have done all we can for her, she could die sometime today".

"Oh, dear God" cried Bridie. "How could this have happened, she is only twenty-one years old, she can't die. What will my mother do, this will kill her"

"I am sorry," he said again as he left.

Mrs Nelson came straight over when she saw the doctor leaving to find Bridie alone and crying. Bridie told Mrs Nelson in between sobs what the doctor had just told her. Mrs Nelson hugged Bridie softly asking where her mother was.

"She is still asleep," Bridie said. "The doctor said she too would be ill if she did not rest, so he gave her another strong sedative last night. How am I ever going to tell her?" cried Bridie

"Listen, Bridie," said Mrs Nelson. "We will get the children up, and I will take them over to our Jane's she is off work today. Then I will come back until Sean comes in from work."

Mrs Nelson was always a tower of strength thought Bridie, thank God I have such good friends like her. The children were as good as gold not asking too many questions as they went with Granny Nelson over to Jane's. Shortly afterwards Mrs Nelson was back to support Bridie and her mother, Maggie. She told Bridie that Jane sent her love and would take care of the children as long as was needed. Dick was going up to see Father Toner and ask him to come and give Margaret the last rites. They could hear Maggie coming down the stairs; Bridie was dreading having to tell her mother the terrible news. When Maggie saw her daughters face, she sensed something was wrong. When Bridie told her what the doctor had said she swayed as if to fall. Mrs Nelson put her arms around her and sat her down on a chair. Mrs Nelson felt so sad for both of them; all she could do was help them in their grief and do what she could for them.

It was a terrible day for all of them, Maggie, Bridie and Sean were at Margaret's bedside when she passed away peacefully and in no pain. Paul, Margaret's fiancé, a handsome young man, arrived later that day but he was too late to see his sweetheart before she died. Paul was devastated; he could not believe what had happened. Sean took him upstairs to see her, a beautiful young girl taken so suddenly. Paul bent down and kissed Margaret, then politely asked Sean to leave him alone with her for a while.

Two days later Margaret was buried in Church Bank cemetery, a long, long way from her home in Dunclare. Maggie was heartbroken; she could not believe that her beautiful young daughter would not be going back home with her to Ireland. While Bridie kept asking herself over and over again why did this tragedy have to happen, her mother had enough sorrow in her life, and now her lovely young sister whom she was so proud of was dead and buried. Margaret had been a ray of sunshine, always happy with everything to live for. She had a good job and a wonderful young man who thought the world of her and she of him. They had made such great plans for their future as man and wife.

"Oh, dear God", Bridie cried, "Why was life so cruel.

Sean and Jane went with Maggie and Paul to Newcastle to see them off on their long journey. Bridie felt she could not bear to watch her mother go; it would be too painful. She wanted to say goodbye at home with the children around her as they helped to ease the ache in her heart.

Chapter 9

It was 1939, three years after her sister's death that Bridie could go back home to see her beloved mother. She would be taking the four youngest children as Margaret had left school and was now working so she would be staying at home with her father. Sean had been saving his pocket money so that Bridie and the children could go for a long holiday with their Granny in Ireland, as Sean knew that Bridie got homesick to see her mother, especially after Margaret's death. Sean and Margaret went with the family to Newcastle to see them on their way, and Sean made sure they were settled in the compartment of the train then kissed them all goodbye. He tried to assure Bridie telling her not to worry about them and to enjoy her stay at home, adding that he would be glad of the peace and quiet but with a twinkle in his eye.

"I am going to miss you all", Sean said to the children. "Give you Granny our love and look after your mother for me". Then he gave Bridie one last kiss and cuddle.

The guard gave the signal that the train was about to leave, Sean and Margaret waved goodbye to the family's sad faces looking through the window. As the train passed out of sight, Sean thought about his own mother who had died four years ago. He would have loved it if she could have seen his family. But Bridie would take them to the house where their Daddy was born to meet their aunts, uncles and cousins. Sean had to stop the tears coming into his eyes as he pictured Bridie and the children blowing kisses as the train pulled away. Bridie felt sad at leaving Sean and Margaret but also happy to be going back home. But it was quite a task trying to keep the children amused on the long train journey. But it was a bigger problem getting off the train and onto the boat with four children and two suitcases. All the children were very tired, only wanting to have a sleep. A young priest who was going home on holiday could see that they needed assistance, he only had a small bag so putting it under his arm picked up Bridie's two suitcases then called to another priest to help them onto the boat. The priests made sure that Bridie and the children were settled on the boat before going off saying they would be back when the boat docked. James and Mary started to feel seasick soon after they sailed out, they had been jumping up and down, looking through the portholes, so Bridie told them to curl up and have a sleep, which they did. The two priests true to their word came to help them off the boat. As it happened, they were from Longford, so they were on the same bus. Bridie was more than grateful for their help and could not thank them enough, but they just shrugged it off, saying they were only too glad to help.

It was another long weary bus journey, so by the time they eventually arrived in Dunclare, Bridie was quite exhausted. Maggie and Tom met them off the bus. Maggie took the baby out of Bridie's tired arms, and Tom carried the suitcases. When they took off their coats, Maggie told them to sit at the table where she had a meal ready for them. The children were quiet as they were surprised when they walked into the house to see the stone floor with no mats and what looked like a big hole in the wall with a fire burning in it and a big black kettle hanging from a hook over the fire. There was no gaslight hanging from the ceiling only a dim lamp on the mantelpiece.

Their Granny looked very old with a long black skirt that went right down to her shoes and a black lace shawl wrapped around her shoulders. Her white hair was in a plait on her head.

"She must be at least a hundred years old", James whispered to Mary.

After they had all eaten, their grandmother said to them, "Come on, be off to bed with you, Bridie you as well", Maggie said looking at her precious daughter. "You look as if you need a good night's sleep. We will have plenty of time tomorrow to talk and catch up with all the news, now goodnight and may God bless you all", as she ushered them all upstairs to bed. The children were all tired but very bemused as they whispered to each other about the strange house. Their mother often spoke to them of her home in Ireland, but they were still surprised at it. But Bridie just smiled as she tucked them up in bed, she already knew what they were thinking by their faces, but she knew too that her children would come to love that old house just as much as she did.

Bridie was right; the children did love the house; they also loved their Granny even though she could be strict with them not like their Mammy. The children had plenty of cousins to play with; they were in and out of each other's houses all day long.

As Bridie and the children would be staying quite a while, it was decided that James and Mary should go to the village school. As well as the usual subjects they learnt how to write and count in Gaelic, which made Bridie very proud of them. But the best part for James and Mary was the new friends that they had made. All Bridie's children were very happy and loved Dunclare their mother's home; they said they wanted to live there forever. The only complaint they had was the buttermilk that Granny would make them drink as they hated the taste of it. Maggie also loved having them all there too, she had other family living around her, but she loved Bridie and the children staying with her as she did not have time to feel lonely or dwell on the past. Bridie too was enjoying every minute of her visit home even though she missed Sean and Margaret very much. Most things were just as she remembered but thanked God people were not as poor as they used to be.

The children would go for long walks with their mother learning about nature, also seeing the places where she went to play as a young girl. The children were fascinated at first having to go to the well for water but were a bit nervous in case they fell in and were never to be seen again. They loved getting a ride on Tommy Connors horse up to the bog and watch the men cut the turf. Tommy would let them have a go at milking the cow; everything was so different and exciting for them. They would play on the giant haystacks with their cousins that were in the field behind their Granny's house. It was so much better thank playing in the back lane at home.

The Ramblers still called at night, but the children would all be in bed before they came. If there was music and dancing the children would creep down the stairs and peep through the bannister rails. Bridie would pretend that she had not seen them as she used to do the same when she was their age, but if Granny saw them, she would chase them back to bed. The children could be there for quite a while before being noticed, although the house was bright through the day with its whitewashed walls it was still quite dark at night as the paraffin lamp did not give off much light.

The village still had its amusing characters, one of them was Bruddy Kelly who had taken over the shop across the way. Bruddy was a handsome devil-me-care type with an Irish smile on his face. Most of the village girls had fallen in love with him at some time or other. He was the only one for miles around who owned a car, with an open-top too, but he always had trouble getting it to start. When all the children were playing, he would say to them, "Would you like a ride in my car?" the children's eyes would light up with all of them shouting, "Yes".

"Well", he would say, "If you give me a push down the hill you can all get in".

The children would all be excited about getting a ride in his car as none of them had ever been in a car before. They would all get behind the car and push until the engine started, but Buddy would be away down the hill laughing and waving his hand, all the children fell for it every time, and none of them ever did get a ride in Bruddy's car.

Bridie took the family to meet their cousins on their Daddy's side, and they stayed there for three nights getting to know and playing on the farm with each other. All the children were blending together as if they had known one another all their lives. When they left, they were made to promise that they would go back to see them.

They returned to Dunclare to be with Granny. Bridie knew the children loved living in Ireland, so she had to keep reminding them that they would have to go back to England shortly as their Daddy was missing them all. But they said they wanted to stay there forever.

Chapter 10

Then suddenly, things changed quickly. War had started between Germany and England. Bridie was worried sick about Sean and Margaret. Sean said for them to stay in Ireland, but Bridie was ill at ease thinking of them, so she decided to go back to Wallsend as soon as possible. Maggie tried to change her daughters' mind saying they would be safer there in Dunclare, but Bridie knew she could not settle thinking that her darling husband and daughter could be in danger. Maggie knew Bridie had made up her mind to go back, so she said, "Why don't you leave James here with me, he loves it here helping Tom with the cattle, and he is doing so well at school?"

"I am sorry ma ma", Bridie said tearfully to her mother. "I know you love him, but I can't leave him, he is still one of my babies I could not bear to be parted from him".

James cringed when he heard his mother calling him a 'baby', wish she would not do that he thought. Even though he loved it in Dunclare and adored his Granny, he also knew he wanted to be where his mother was. Bridie felt so sad at leaving her mother, but she knew in her heart that she had to get back to Wallsend. The war would not last long so that the whole family would be back for a holiday next year. The children too were very sad leaving their Granny, cousins and friends but still were excited at the thought of seeing their Daddy again. Maggie hid her tears from the children as they got onto the Dublin bus, she hugged her darling daughter saying she would pray to God and his blessed mother to keep them all safe.

The boat was crowded, as usual, everyone was issued with a life jacket, of course, this made the passengers quite worried as it meant that they could be bombed as they sailed over the rough seas. Everyone was quiet not like it usually is, there was a tense feeling all over the boat, so some young men started to sing. One of them sang a song unknown to Bridie, but it was to stay in all of the family's mind for years to come. It went...

My ship sails tonight love

My darling my dear and

Our meeting at last it is o'er

If you love me as true

As you once used to do

Will you meet me tonight

Love onshore

At last, their long journey was over, and they arrived in Newcastle on a cold, wet morning. They struggled along the road for their tram to Wallsend. Bridie now wished that she had told Sean that they would be back today as he would have come to the station to meet them, but at the time she thought she would surprise him and Margaret. They were just turning the corner of their street when a young man in a sailor's uniform offered to help them. Bridie thanked him then she realised he was one of the Hindmarch boys who lived a few doors away from them

"I didn't recognise you Jack in that uniform. Have you joined the navy?"

"I have been called up", Jack replied. "So have a lot of the other lads in our street. We are waiting for orders to go overseas".

It was at that moment Bridie realised how serious it all was then she gave a silent prayer that it would all end soon. Bridie tried the front door of their home; it was not locked.

"Someone must be in", Bridie said to her very tired children.

Then Margaret came running down the stairs all excited to see them. She could not believe that they were back home. Margaret rushed to her mother throwing her arms around her neck saying, "Why didn't you tell us you would be home today? I could have had a meal ready for you. Wait until dad gets home, boy he will be surprised".

Bridie was amazed at how grown-up Margaret looked. Her firstborn was now a beautiful young woman with a smart little figure and what is all this fancy talk, what was that she said 'oh boy' I have never heard her talk like that before. She must have heard some film star say it at the pictures. Also, it is dad now, not daddy.

By seven o'clock, the children were all in bed fast asleep as they were so tired after their long journey. Bridie was sitting talking to Margaret telling her all about her Granny and everyone back home in Dunclare when Sean walked in. There was a shocked look of disbelief on his face when he saw Bridie, but then his face lit up with that smile that Bridie loved so much.

"Bridie me darlin", Sean said, as he held his arms out to embrace her. He held her in his arms as if he was never going to let her go again.

"It's so good to see you", Sean said. "How are my youngsters, are they all in bed?"

"They were far too tired to stay up", Bridie replied.

"I'm sure they were", Sean said, "But I will just pop upstairs to see them. I can't tell you how happy I am to see you and have you all back again".

Sean gave Bridie another kiss then went quietly up the stairs to see his children.

The family soon settled down now that they were back in Wallsend. The children had lots to tell their friends about Ireland and of all the things that they did. Catherine was now old enough to start work while James and Mary went back to school. Margaret was doing well in her job at the grocery store while Sean was still working hard down the mine. It was less than two weeks after coming home when a loud knock at the front door woke Mary up. She went downstairs to find it was a telegram boy with a telegram for her mother. Mary ran upstairs, jumped on her mother's bed and handed it to Bridie. As Bridie's trembling hands opened it, Mary watched her mother as she started to cry, oh no oh dear God no, then put her hands over her face sobbing.

"What's the matter Mammy?" asked Mary moving closer to her mother feeling very confused.

"It's your Granny, she has just died", said Bridie quietly with tears falling down her cheeks.

The whole family were so sad at losing their Granny as she had been so well when they left her. Bridie felt broken-hearted and so helpless as there was nothing she could do as she could not possibly get over home for her mother's funeral. Two days later a letter arrived from Tom. He had found his mother in bed; she had died in her sleep. They all thought she had died of a broken heart as she had missed Bridie and the children so much. Bridie felt her own heart was breaking too after losing her beloved mother but with her own family to care for and worry about, also with this terrible war going on she knew her mother would not want her to mourn for her and would want them to get on with their lives. Bridie knew her mother would always be in her heart and prayers; she would also keep her memory alive by talking about her to the family as they had loved their Granny too.

The war situation was getting worse; there seemed to be no end to it. Air-raid shelters were built in back gardens and front streets. Air-raid sirens would go most nights when people were in bed. Bridie would have to wake the children out of their sleep to go into the shelter. Sean stayed in bed as he needed his sleep as he would have to go to work because it would be too dangerous going down the mine tired. The shelters were cold and damp, so Bridie made sure that the family had plenty of warm clothing on. The younger children wore all-in-one suits made mostly of old blankets like other children people named them siren-suits. Everyone was issued with a gas-mask; they were in a cardboard box with a string so that it could be carried on your shoulder. There were no windows in the shelters, so the only light they had were from candles, so there was always the smell of candle grease plus the damp smell off the concrete walls.

It was a terrible ordeal, especially for people with children. Every night for five long years, not knowing whether they would be killed by a bomb as their houses were quite close to the shipyard. Sometimes the sirens would go during the day when the children were at school. The children would be frightened and cry for their mothers while the mothers would want to run to the school to be with their children. At night there were no streetlights on, so it was very dark outside, a lot of people carried torches. Windows of houses had to be blacked out by thick curtains or dark paper blinds. The home-guard would patrol the streets if a flicker of light were showing they would bang on the front door shouting a warning to cover the window. It was a serious offence; you could be fined or jailed if it happened too many times. Almost all food and clothing were rationed, even sweets, a ration book was issued to everyone. You were allowed so much each week, and you only got small amounts, there was no way that you could get anything if you spent your rations. Fruit too was very scarce. You stood in a queue for maybe some oranges only to find when it was almost your turn to be served, they were sold out, it was very disappointing and frustrating.

Many of the children were evacuated, staying with families in the country, but Sean and Bridie refused to let their children go. What would it do to them being sent away to live with complete strangers? There was no question about it; they would all stay together as a family should. Apart from children being evacuated and most of the men joining the armed forces life went on as usual with people struggling to feed their families on the meagre rations allotted to them. Most of the women baked their own bread, some being taught by neighbours who knew how to bake it.

James had now left school and started work in Swans shipyard as an apprentice joiner. So that left Mary and Patrick still at school. The other girls spent all their pocket money on clothes, make-up and going to dances. They went every Friday night to the Tara club in Newcastle where they danced to the Irish bands as most of the people were Irish. Then on a Saturday night, they would go to the Oxford Galleries and Wallsend Memorial Hall for modern dancing. When there was a Ceili dance in the Parochial Hall Bridie and Jane would go with them.

The Lavin's house was always filled with laughter as all the family's friends were always made very welcome. Sylvia and Joyce called almost every night of the week. The girls would all wash their hair then they would set each other's so a lot of chit-chat went on. Every month or so they would ask Bridie to tell them their fortune, she would tell the cards or read their tea leaves. They would believe every word she said, and Sylvia was always hoping there would be a tall, dark stranger somewhere in them. The girls would tell Bridie all about the dances and of boyfriends they may have. Sean did not mind the family's friends all being there as he knew Bridie and Jane enjoyed listening to them and having a good laugh. Sean was a great reader; every night, he would enjoy reading a good book. A lot of them would be cowboy stories so he would be quite content smoking his pipe and reading.

Sean's brother Peter and his wife Annie would come down from Scotland, other times their sons Patrick, Michael and James would come for a weekend. Bridie always made room for them as they all loved their Scottish relations coming. The boys were all good singers and knew every Irish song ever written. It was one long party when they came down.

If it were a nice summers evening, they would have a singsong in the back lane. The neighbours would sit around the back-lane doors listening to them singing or join in with the songs they knew. They would be there until one o'clock in the morning, everybody just having a real good time. Then other weekends James and the girls would go to Scotland for a weekend. James was now a handsome young man and football was his and his friends only interest. They went to see Newcastle United play at every opportunity. Football was more important than girlfriends to them.

Bridie still had a great sense of Irish humour, one frosty evening she went into the back yard to fetch in a sheet that was on the clothesline, it was frozen stiff, so she lifted it off the line with the clothes prop. Some young lads who were in the back lane saw the sheet lifting up, one of them said look there is a ghost, so Bridie lifted the sheet higher, then made an 'eerie' sound 'ooh ooh', and they all fled down the dark lane. The following day they were telling everyone about the ghost they had seen, Bridie let them go on for a while then she told them it was her to their relief.

Friday night was usually quiet in the Lavin's house. The girls would be at a dance, James and Mary would go to the pictures with their friends so when Patrick was in bed there was nothing that Sean and Bridie liked better than to listen to the radio or 'wireless' as it was called. It was very relaxing to sit by themselves by the fireside and listen to some music or a good play 'Cavan O'Connor' would sing lovely Irish songs. He was known as the 'strolling vagabond'. They also enjoyed the man in black or Dick Barton special agent. At lunchtime there was 'workers playtime' many singers and comedians became household names after being on this programme.

Wallsend Park was a popular place to go. The brass band played there every Sunday afternoon. Families would take a picnic, and sweethearts would stroll around holding hands while the children all wanted to feed the ducks and swans.

In the winter evenings, the women would pass the time making 'clippie mats. They would use old hessian sugar bags for the backing then draw on their own pattern using old clothing cut into strips, making them very colourful. It would take a few weeks to make one. Usually, all the family would take a part in making it, all of them being very proud of the piece they had created. Bridie always made a new one for Christmas. It would be put down at the fireplace on Christmas Eve while the old one would have been washed then put in the scullery.

A lot of people enjoyed having a gamble and Bridie was no exception. She enjoyed playing cards and having a flutter on the horses. She would study the form in the 'Sporting man paper', her stakes were never very high, she would have a sixpence each-way bet, but she always bet on the Irish horses. There were no betting shops so Mr Hancock at the top of the street would take the bets, he had to be careful as it was illegal for him to take them. He would have someone to be his 'lookout' in case the police arrived in the street.

In the summer, on a Saturday, some of the men would play cards in the back lane. Also, the men coming home from the pub would play 'pitch and toss'. The card players only played with coppers, but the 'pitch and toss' men were hardened gamblers, so they played for half-a-crown. They too had a look-out-man, if a policeman did appear the men would scatter in all directions into anyone's house saying the coppers are in the lane then they would apologise for their intrusion before leaving by the front door. People would help each other; they did not think anything of it. Sean always made a joke about it all saying Bridie would take pity on the devil himself.

The back lane was where all the children played as the air raid shelters were in the front street. The grown-ups would often join in their games such as rounders, skipping or four sticks. The young girls would play 'Bays' with an old polish tin or 'Buttony'. This game was to flick your button on to your friends' button then you would win that button, they always had their favourite button. The boys would play marbles; they too had their favourites.

On a Sunday afternoon, a 'Vagabond' would sing in the front street, a lot of them were very good singers, so they hoped to make a few pennies. Bridie always sent one of the children out with a penny if he sang an Irish song. Another pastime was going to the pictures, it only cost a couple of pence, and it took their minds off the war that was going on. The film would often snap just at the exciting part then you would have to wait until it was put right again. But all the young lads would stamp their feet in frustration until it was fixed then they would settle down to enjoy the film until it snapped again. Bridie would take Mary and Patrick every week. Sean only went once to the pictures, and that was to see 'Old Mother Riley', but the whole family would go once a month to the theatre either to the Empire or Palace to see a live show in Newcastle.

Bridie often thought of her home back in Ireland. Also, her mother and father would be in her prayers. Every night the family too would talk about their stay with their Granny in their 'magic' village of Dunclare. Tom had taken over his mother's house, making it and his own into one house. He often wrote to Bridie saying that when the war was over, he would love to have them all go over as there was plenty of room for all of them. Danny too still wrote from America, always sending a few dollars, the children loved to boast about their

Uncle being in the American Police Force just like they saw in the films.

There had been rumours that the war would soon be over. When it was eventually announced on the wireless everyone was jubilant. Margaret came into the house saying, "Come on, everyone is going down to the town hall".

Sean just sat reading his book as Bridie and the family put on their coats and went down the street meeting neighbours coming out of their houses all making their way toward the town hall that was just at the bottom of their street. The Lord Mayor came onto the balcony and announced that the war was over. Everyone cheered then a great big bonfire was lit, the faces of the people was a sight to behold all smiling as men women and children danced around the fire. That night in Bridie's prayers she thanked God for keeping them safe during the war years, then she prayed for the souls of all the young men on both sides of the war who had lost their lives.

Chapter 11

It was three years after the war that Sean and Bridie started making plans to go back home for a holiday. Tom was always asking them to go over as he never went on holiday; his excuse was he could not leave the cattle. Bridie wrote to Tom telling him that they would be over in the summer for a couple of weeks taking Mary, who was now fourteen and Patrick, who was nine. The three oldest were working and could take care of themselves. James, who was now eighteen, was a handsome young man and enjoyed being a trainee joiner, he was also taking driving lessons. He gave his mother most of his wages as she was helping him to save for a car.

"The first thing that I am going to do Mam when I pass my test and get a car is to take you for a run into the country", he said.

"That will be great son", said Bridie feeling so proud that her son could drive a car as no one in their street had one.

There was something that Bridie had been concerned about for a while. James had been having a lot of pain in his stomach. The doctor assured her that there was no need to worry as most young people get aches and pains; it was all part of growing up. But Bridie could not help worrying over him. At one visit to the doctor, Bridie said, "Surely it's not natural for James to go to bed early with pain when he should be out with his friends enjoying himself?"

The doctor said he would make an appointment at the hospital for James to have some tests done. A week before Easter, James went into Hexham General Hospital, the hospital was miles away into the country. Sean and Bridie were worried sick about their darling son as the hospital was known to have a lot of T.B. patients. After a long wait, the doctor came to see them; he said the x-rays showed that James did not have T.B.

"Oh, thank God," said Bridie "I have been so worried about him".

"Yes", replied the doctor, "It is good news, but I would still like to keep your son here for another few days to have some more tests done".

The doctor could see by Bridie's face she was still very worried.

"I am sure everything will be alright Mrs Lavin, it's just that seeing you have come all this way to our hospital we may as well try and find what is causing James to have all this pain".

Sean went with his son to the ward while Bridie went to the hospital shop to buy James a bottle of Lucozade and sweets. When Bridie got back to the ward, James was already in bed. He looks like a small boy again thought Bridie as she kissed her son goodbye telling him that she would phone the hospital tomorrow from the phone box on Wallsend high street. Bridie phoned every day that week to ask how James was. They told her that he would be home at the weekend but that he would have to return on the Tuesday. The whole family were in the house waiting for him when he arrived in an ambulance. They had all missed him so much as the house was so quiet now, James was always fooling around tormenting them all. They also felt that they should not be enjoying themselves while he was in the hospital.

Bridie put her arms around James and gave him a big hug. She thought her dear son had lost weight, but maybe she was imagining it. After a while, all James wanted to do was to have a game of football. His pals were still at work, so he asked his Dad if he fancied a game in the back lane

"I don't think you should son", said Bridie, "Remember you have just come out of hospital".

"Leave the boy alone", said Sean kissing his wife on her cheek. "You worry too much; he will be alright, come on, son."

Then as they were going out, James kissed his mother, saying, "I'm alright Mam honestly".

They were only out a short while when James told his father that he was too tired to play anymore. Sean made sure they went straight into the house; Bridie got a pillow and blanket for James to have a lay down on the settee.

The following day James never mentioned going to play football. His pals all called to see him, they played darts and had a game of cards while Bridie was kept busy making sandwiches for them all. The weekend was over before they knew it. On the Tuesday, Sean and Bridie travelled back with their son to the hospital. They asked the doctor what they intended to do.

"We are taking x-rays and may have to operate on James to find out what is causing all his pain. But do not worry, I am sure he will be fine, it could be a small blockage in the bowel which a small operation will cure it".

It was with a heavy heart that Sean and Bridie left their son in the hands of the doctors while they returned back to their home in Wallsend. Bridie could not concentrate on anything because she just could not get James out of her mind; she was terribly worried about him even though the doctor had assured them that he would be alright.

James went through his operation on the Thursday, both Sean and Bridie were there, waiting for him when he came out of the theatre. He did not go back to the big ward but had a nice little room of his own. Bridie was sitting holding her dear son's hand waiting for him to open his eyes when a young nurse came quietly into the room saying to them, "It will be a while before James comes around so the doctor would like a word with you in his office".

Sean and Bridie followed the nurse along the corridor to see the doctor.

"Please sit down", the doctor beckoned as he closed the door behind them. Bridie had a terrible feeling in her stomach; she could not take her eyes off the doctor wondering what he was going to say to them. The doctor sat on the edge of his desk in front of Sean and Bridie then looking straight at them said, "I am very sorry, but I have very sad news to tell you".

Those words would forever be ringing in Bridie's ears until the day she died. Sean clasped his dear wife's hand as they waited for the doctor to speak again.

"I am sorry to have to tell you that your son has bowel cancer and there is nothing that we can for him".

Bridie and Sean sat dazed; they could not speak or look at each other for a few seconds. Then Sean asked the doctor how many years James would have and would he be able to lead a normal life. The doctor realising that they were in shock and did not understand how serious it all was, stood up and taking both their hands, told them, as gently as he could, that James would live for four weeks at the most.

"Oh, dear God in heaven please don't let this be happening to us", cried Bridie, while Sean was crying "Sweet Jesus not our James", as they clung to each other broken-hearted.

Sean and Bridie stayed at the hospital all day sitting at their son's bedside, waiting for him to wake up. They told the doctor not to tell James about his illness as they wanted him to spend the rest of his life as happy as they could make it for him. It was the longest journey that Sean and Bridie had ever taken in their life going back from the hospital to Wallsend. Their hearts were broken and were dreading having to tell the family the dreadful news about their brother. The two oldest girls were still up waiting for them to come home. Sean, with his tear-stained face, broke the sad news to them. It was in the middle of the night that Mary now fourteen could hear her mother sobbing, she crept into bed beside her and asked what was wrong, but Bridie could not answer her young daughter.

"Please Mam", said Mary, "What is the matter? Is it our James, is he not well?"

Bridie put her arm around Mary and held her close whispering, "It's our James, he has cancer, he only has a few weeks to live", as she sobbed into the pillow.

Mary, like the rest of the family, was broken-hearted, she dreaded bedtime as she could hear her mother crying every night when she thought everyone was asleep. How Bridie lived through the following weeks no-one would ever know. Her heart was broken, and she wanted to die herself, how could she go on living without her darling son.

The nurses at the hospital had taken James into their hearts as he was such a good patient, so they spoilt him rotten. Even though the journey to the hospital was very tiring, Bridie went to see James every day. She wanted to spend all the time she could with her precious son. At the weekends all the family would go, James never questioned about what was wrong with him he just took it for granted that he would go home when the doctor said he could. After all, it takes weeks to recover from an operation. Some days James was able to get out of bed he would take a walk into the other wards. When he was too tired to get out of bed, a lot of the patients he had made friends with would go along to see him. James had his nineteenth birthday in the hospital, the nurses who cared for him decorated his room with lovely, coloured balloons. All the family were there with him to celebrate, hiding their sadness, knowing this would be his last birthday.

James dies on the 19th April; Sean Bridie and the two oldest girls were at his bedside at the end of his young life.

Although Bridie knew she had a devoted husband and wonderful family, she could not get over the death of her son. She was losing all interest in life; her beautiful auburn hair turned grey almost overnight. The family too were all so sad they felt it would be wrong to laugh, sing or even talk about James. The family missed their mother's happy smiling face as she would always be singing around the house but that all stopped the day that the doctor at the hospital told them the devastating news about James. Jane would try to console her dear friend; she was always there for her. Then at night when the girl's friends would come, they would sit quietly talking about their clothes, make-up etc. But now there was no laughter and fun like there used to be.

The young curate from church Father White called in regularly to see Bridie. She would say that it was he who made her see that life had to go on even though her heart was breaking. One day after he had been to see her, she thought about his comforting words and felt that God had been speaking through him. Was she being selfish, she thought, only thinking of her own heartache, what about Sean did she ever think of how he felt losing his son? Also, the rest of the family they had lost a brother they had loved dearly. Bridie realised that Sean and their family needed her now more than ever so she would try to be less self-centred and get on with life. Bridie's life did go on, but her darling son James would never be far away from her thoughts and prayers.

Chapter 12

The family life of the Lavin's did go on; the three girls loved dancing and going over to Ireland for their holidays. Patrick was a great rock and roll fan, Elvis Presley being his idol. While the girls all went to modern dancing in the Oxford and Old Assembly rooms. But their favourite was the Ceili dancing, going every Friday night to the Tara club. The girls all married Irish men, from Mayo, Roscommon and Armagh. Patrick married a local girl from Wallsend.

The family soon started having their own families, so Bridie and Sean even on their own now were never short of company. They had eighteen grandchildren, most of them were born in their own home, and Bridie was always there when she was called upon to be at the births. The midwife too was always glad of her assistance. Bridie would leave whatever she was doing when she was needed by her family, and of course, she was called upon quite often. The grandchildren all loved going to 'Nannas' house, they loved her cooking and the wonderful stories she would tell them. Sean would sit in his chair reading a book and smoking his pipe while Bridie was telling them a story as she did with their own children. Sean would smile at the remarks his grandchildren would come out with then he would wink at Bridie as he lifted one of them into the air amid shrieks of excitement.

Shortly Sean would be retiring from the Rising Sun Colliery where he had worked for fifty years. He would then have more time to spend in his allotment where he kept hens and grew vegetables of all kind for all the family. He had a great interest in growing prize leeks and onions. He won many prizes with them and with his flowers, Dahlias being his favourite. Sean's flowers were always admired by passers-by, needless to say; he always gave them a bunch.

Sean had always been blessed with good health, so it was a terrible shock for Bridie when one morning, she found that Sean had died in his sleep. The coal dust had taken its toll, and another miner had died as a result of it. Bridie tried to console herself by thanking God that he did not suffer too much and that he had died peacefully in his own home, the one and only home that they shared together. All the family rallied around their mother, each one wanting her to go and live with them. Bridie knew she had the best family in the world, she knew they were all worried about her living on her own, but she wanted to spend the rest of her life in her own home and reassured her family she would be just fine. Bridie had all her memories in that house, her and Sean starting married life, where all their children were born, the home where they had so many happy times with family and friends but alas some very sad ones too.

Bridie missed Sean terribly, especially at night when she was along with her thoughts of their life together. Also, of their beloved son James who had died at such a very young age. In the daylight hours, things were so different as she had the company of her family calling. Jane, Bridie's oldest and true friend, would call in for a cup of tea and tell her all the gossip. They often reminisced of the good times they had when they worked together all those years ago, and they enjoyed a good laugh together. Jane had been on her own quite a while now, but with no family of her own, she had a lot of time to herself, so she often went over to Ireland to spend time with her cousins.

Bridie looked forward to her letters from Tom and Eileen back home, also from Danny in Chicago. Danny still sent her a few dollars in his letters. The family were all excited when their mother told them that Danny was to go back to Dunclare in the summer for a holiday and asking her if she would be over too. It had been a long time since she was home, she never wanted a holiday again after her dear son had died, but now her daughters were planning everything for her so she could not refuse. Catherine, Mary and granddaughter Geraldine were to go over with her to see her brother Danny who had left home fifty years ago. This was his first time back home. They decided it would be better to fly over then they would hire a car over in Ireland. Bridie was not in the best of health having chest problems, but you never heard her complaining.

"Will you be alright going by air Nanna?" asked Geraldine, knowing her Nanna had never flown before.

"I will probably be terrified", laughed Bridie "But I am willing to fly this one time just to see our Danny".

The day soon came around when they were off to Ireland, the girls being as excited as their mother. When they were on the plane up in the air, Geraldine asked her Nanna if she was alright and enjoying the flight.

"Yes it's fine love", said Bridie forcing a big smile. She later told them when they were back in Newcastle that she had been terrified and would never fly again. But that was Bridie; she always put on a brave face; she was never a selfish woman and would not want her family to be worried about her.

It was late afternoon when they arrived at Dublin airport. Their train down to Roscommon would not be due until early evening, so they went into Dublin centre and had tea in a nice little café in O'Connell street before taking a taxi to the railway station. While waiting on the platform, Catherine was surprised to see Amy and Rosie O'Neill, her husband's nieces from Castlerea. Amy and Rosie worked in Marks and Spencer's in Dublin; they shared a small flat in Dublin but always went home at weekends. It was lovely meeting them, so there was plenty to talk about on their journey down.

It was a dark stormy night when the train arrived at the small railway station in Castlerea. Bridie had butterflies in her tummy at the thought of being back home in Co. Roscommon again. Bridie, Catherine, Mary and Geraldine were the only ones apart from the O'Neill girls to get off the train.

Amy said, "Daddy will be waiting for us in the car. If you stand in out of the rain, I will tell him that you are here, I am sure he will want to see you".

The girls and Bridie went quickly out of the rain into the small dimly lit waiting room. Geraldine said, "We should have hired a car when we arrived in Dublin, it would have been more sensible", they all agreed with her.

Then Tommy O'Neill came rushing into the waiting room the rain dripping off his jet-black hair. "Hello Catherine, it's nice to see you again", he said, shaking her hand.

"Hello Tommy, it's great to be back again", then she introduced him to her companions.

"I had heard that your mother was coming back home", he said looking at Bridie, his smile lighting up his ruggedly handsome face. "You know what it's like here, news spreads itself just like the devil himself".

"What are your plans? Are you going down to Dunclare tonight?" Tommy asked.

"Well you see Tommy we have come a day earlier than planned or someone would have met us, we are staying with our Tom", said Bridie, adding, "But as it is so late we thought we would spend tonight in a hotel then go down to Dunclare in the morning".

"Well you have certainly picked a nice night to arrive, it's been raining all day long. I am sure you must all be tired", he said, looking at Bridie.

"If you stay here in the waiting room, I will come back for you after I drop the two girls off. There is a nice house just up the road Mrs Owen will make you very welcome I am sure. I will be back in fifteen minutes", he shouted as he ran through the rain to his car.

Bridie and the girls sat down on the wooden bench in the draughty waiting room for Tommy to return. The girls were worried about their mother as she looked very pale and tired; they were wishing they were all in bed and settled for the night.

"What a lovely man Tommy is, it's a blessing that he was here at the station", Bridie said.

"Yes, he is", replied Catherine, "He has a lovely nature, he would run a mile for anyone. Thank God he was here as this place as it is in the wilds of nowhere. There is no sign of a telephone, but this is Ireland what we know and love, I suppose it's what holidaymakers call the "charm of the place" Even though they were all cold and tired they had a good laugh about it.

Tommy true to his word came back for them, he helped them to the car then drove through the blinding rain to the boarding house. He introduced them to Mrs Owen, the landlady; then he took their cases upstairs. Mrs Owen showed them a brightly lit bedroom with two double beds.

"Now, will this do for you? I hope you don't mind sharing as this is the only room, I have vacant", she said.

"This will do lovely", Bridie said looking around the bright, pleasant room.

"Well, I am sure you must be dying for a nice cup of tea, I will go down and make it for you. Make yourselves comfortable I will bring it up for you".

Then Tommy said goodnight to them all saying he would come for them in the morning. Mrs Owen brought them up a pot of tea and a plate of delicious ham sandwiches, then she bade them goodnight saying she hoped they would sleep well. They were all very tired after their long journey, so after they had their tea, they all went straight to bed. The beds were lovely and comfortable, so it wasn't long before they were all fast asleep.

Daybreak dawned, and Bridie lay there looking at the bright sunshine beaming through the window. The girls were still fast asleep. Poor kids Bridie thought to herself, they must have been shattered. I'll let them sleep awhile longer, there's no need to wake them up yet. Bridie lay there thinking she was very excited at the thought of meeting her brother Danny after so many years. Memories also came flooding back into her mind of their childhood and the hard times they had suffered. But her thoughts were of her dear Mother who had struggled so hard to bring them all up, also of Danny and how would he feel coming home after fifty long years. Bridie got up out of bed saying to herself that they had a lot of happy times too so enough of these sad thoughts this was going to be a happy reunion for them all.

After Bridie had knelt down and said her morning prayers, she got washed and dressed before waking up the girls. She then went downstairs to find it was a lovely morning, especially after the terrible storm the night before. When the girls came downstairs, they all went into the dining room where Mrs Owen had a lovely, cooked breakfast for them, making sure they had enough to eat with as much tea or coffee they wanted.

They had just finished breakfast when Tommy arrived, "Good morning, did you all sleep well?" he asked with that smile still on his handsome face.

"Yes, we all had a good night's sleep and feel much better this morning," said Bridie. "I don't know what we would have done without you, Tommy, you're a darlin".

Tommy looking embarrassed said, "Not at all sure it was no trouble, I'm glad I was able to help. Well what do you want to do first, I can run you to Dunclare if you want", he said.

"The first thing we need is a car. Is there somewhere we can hire one for the week?" said Geraldine.

"No problem", replied Tommy. "If you are ready, I will take you to Paul Lynch's garage; he has some good cars it's only a couple of miles up the road".

The girls and Bridie were quite nervous sitting in Tommy's car as he went speeding along the narrow country lanes never slowing down at road junctions. As he was telling them, he had been driving over twenty years, and he had never taken a driving test. "I have never thought about it", he said. "I suppose I will take one of these days," he said laughing.

They arrived in one piece at the garage. Bridie and the girls were thankful to get out of Tommy's car, they made good-humoured remarks about his driving, but Tommy just laughed it off. Nothing seemed to worry him; he was such a happy-go-lucky sort of chap. Tommy was pleased with the deal the girls got at the garage for the red Renault 5 car they hired. Bridie and the girls settled themselves in the car then Tommy pointed out directions of how to get to Dunclare. The village of Dunclare was almost five-mile away so as they drove along Bridie was amazed and maybe a little disheartened that a lot of the thatched cottages were gone and, in their place, lovely new houses.

The girls were getting excited at seeing their uncle Danny from America whom they had heard so much about, but they were more excited for Bridie. It was also special for Geraldine to be going to the village that she had heard so much about, where Nanna lived as a child also her own mother Mary had told her all about the village she also had loved and even went to school there herself. When they reached the village, Bridie pointed out to Geraldine the house to go to.

Tom Donnelly opened the door of the house when he had heard the car pull up outside. He was all smiles as he kissed his sister, then shook hands with the girls.

"We were not expecting you until this evening", he said as they all walked in. He took their coats then beckoned them to sit down.

The girls were looking around the room, trying to picture their Grannys house, but everything looked so different. Tom realised what they were thinking, told them he had made a lot of alterations since he made his house and his mother house into one home. Bridie looked around trying to visualise the home she was brought up in but could not, it was so different. Now there were carpets on the floor, modern furniture and in place of the open turf fire was a wooden surround fireplace with an electric fire and electric lights too. The back of the house where the turf used to be stacked was now a lovely modern kitchen. The only thing that Bridie was familiar with and was very happy to see was the same sacred heart photo hanging over the fireplace.

"There have been many changes since you were here last Bridie", said Tom putting his arm around her shoulder.

"Yes, there certainly has. By the way", Bridie asked, "Where is everyone?"

Tom told her that Danny had taken Eileen into Derrymacash to do some shopping, adding that Danny had hired a car in Dublin when he arrived. "He will be disappointed that he wasn't here to greet you, but we thought you were arriving tonight, he was going to meet you at the station. Come on upstairs, Tom said, I will show you where you are all sleeping, then I will make you a cup of tea. Eileen will be making you a meal when she comes in, they shouldn't be too long".

Bridie and the girls were chatting away to Tom when they heard a car pulling up outside. "Here they are now", Tom said, smiling at Bridie as he went to open the door. Bridie followed Tom to the door and saw this tall, distinguished grey-haired man looking toward them. He looked at Bridie, knowing this was his big sister even though he had not seen her since he was a child. Bridie walked into his outstretched arms, both of them with tears of mixed emotions in their eyes. The girls too had tears of happiness for both of them, together again after so many years apart. They had heard their mother talk so much of their uncle Danny in America and now he was here.

Eileen had a lovely meal ready for them in no time, and everyone was soon telling each other all about their families with photographs being taken by the girls. The two men with Bridie and Eileen started to reminisce of when they were young. The girls enjoyed listening to them, even though they had heard most of their stories before, from their mother. Also, that Ireland was the best country in the world. The girls thought how alert their minds were for their age, the four of them all getting on in years, but their memories were marvellous. Tom asked the girls if they would like to go out for a drink, but they declined, they were all happy talking about old times.

"No thanks, Uncle Tom", said Mary. "We are going to have an early night."

"It might be a wise thing to do", Tom said, "Because tomorrow the whole family will be here, so God only knows what time we will get to bed. But have a nightcap before you go. What are you having girls?" still with that mischievous twinkle in his eye.

Next morning over breakfast, the girls were asking their uncle Danny about his life in America, they were also enjoying his sense of humour just like their mother. Then after breakfast Danny, Bridie and the girls decided to go out for a walk around the village as it was such a beautiful morning. The first place they headed for was to the well, that is to say where the well, used to be, now it was covered in, with lovely rose bushes at the bottom of someone's garden.

"Do you remember Bridie the times we would carry a

bucket of water from the well for Ma Ma, but half of it would be spilt out by the time we reached back home?" asked Danny.

"Yes", laughed Bridie, "Do you remember old Mrs Higgins, she would give us an old, bruised apple for fetching her a couple of buckets of water".

The girls were so happy to see their mother and Uncle Danny talking of old times. They were in a world of their own enjoying being together after fifty long years, even though they wrote to each other quite often, so they decided to leave them on their own and have a wander up to the church. Mary showed her daughter Geraldine the old school or what was left of it where she had gone to as a child. Geraldine was very interested in everything. She had, at last, come to Dunclare the village her grandmother Bridie had told her so much about. Also, where her mother Mary, had spent a special part of her childhood.

After lunch, the girls helped Eileen to make sandwiches etc. When the food was laid out on the table, it looked very appetising, and Tom had made sure that there was plenty to drink too. The families started to arrive mid-afternoon, so the house was quite full, with everyone talking and laughing, it was lovely. The brothers and sisters together again, also friends called in the evening it was just like old times with plenty of yarns being told. Danny was the first to sing a song; everyone said he missed his vocation as he had a lovely singing voice. The merriment went on until two-thirty then someone said it was past their bedtime so they should be making their way back to home.

Tom, Danny, Eileen, Bridie and the girls went outside to wave to them as they left in their cars, then they all rushed back into the house out of the cold night air.

The girls told them to get to bed and that they would wash up and put everything away. It did not take them very long to have the place nice and tidy again. Then they were very glad to roll into bed themselves.

The next couple of days it poured down with rain, it was far too wet to go anywhere, so they all spent the time talking, reading, playing cards or watching television. There was no such thing now as the 'Ramblers" calling to tell stories or have a set dance in people's houses as television had spoilt all that.

One day Bridie and the girls went to visit Tommy and Theresa O'Neill. They spent a lovely day with them and their family. Tommy was pleased that the car they had hired had been trouble-free for them. Before they left Geraldine said she would go and turn the car around, she opened the front door then cried "Dear God".

"What is the matter with you?" Mary asked her daughter.

Geraldine said, "I can't see anything; everything is black".

Mary's heart almost stopped beating as she rushed towards her daughter, taking hold of her arm, saying, "What do you mean you can't see?"

"Look", said Geraldine, "You can't see a thing outside it's so dark", she said quite innocently.

Mary gave a big sigh of relief as she thought her daughter had lost her sight. Then having looked outside herself it was so true; it was pitch dark as they were way out in the country with not one sign of light anywhere. Before they left, they asked Tommy and Theresa if they would like to have a day out with them the following day as their Uncle Danny wanted to have a run-out with them.

"Great", said Theresa, "We haven't been anywhere for a long time, sure I think we deserve a break", she said looking at Tommy with a pleading look on her face. "Joe and Dan can take care of things; we will take Jane and Rosie with us",

"Why not", said Tommy putting his arm around his lovely wife. "A day out will do us no harm at all".

"Right", said Bridie. "Why don't you call for us around eleven o'clock?"

"That will do us fine", said Theresa.

The following morning, they all set out for the day to Lough Key Forest Park, it was a beautiful sunny morning, and Danny was enjoying every minute of his run out with some of his family. Forest Park was a lovely place to go for a day out. The two young children were excited about being in the rowing boats on the lake. While everyone else was enjoying the lovely surroundings, playing games with the children and everyone having had ice cream. Everyone had tired themselves out before returning back home.

The following day Danny went off to visit his wife's brother, so the girls and Bridie went to Boyle to see cousins of Sean's. They lived in a lovely spot on the outskirts of Boyle. Bridie still remembered how to get there. Peggy and Tommy O'Rourke had a lovely home with a lovely garden surrounding it, and they were delighted to see their unexpected visitors. Peggy made them all a very tasty lunch which they had outside on the lawn. After spending a lovely day with them, they decided it was time to leave even though Peggy and Tommy wanted them to spend the night with them.

They said their goodbyes and drove along at a leisurely pace just enjoying the lovely countryside around them. They stopped at a small hotel for a cup of tea but could not resist the home-baked scones with lashings of cream on top.

Mary thought her mother looked very tired, so she suggested that they spend the night in the hotel. They all thought this was a good idea. So they booked in at the front desk, then they were shown upstairs to two rooms with twin beds. The rooms were clean and comfortable, and they all enjoyed having a lovely hot bath before going downstairs for dinner. After dinner, they phoned Tom to let him know what they were doing. Then they talked about going out to a pub to see if there was any Irish music as there was none in the hotel. Bridie was too tired to go out anywhere she just wanted to get to bed and maybe have a read, but she said to the girls to get themselves out and make the most of it as they would be leaving in a couple of days. The girls felt guilty leaving Bridie alone, but they knew she was really tired so they saw to it that she was tucked up in bed looking very comfortable with her sweets and magazines that Geraldine had gone out and bought for her before they ventured out into this small town.

It was already getting dark when the girls left the hotel, and they noticed how quiet the place was as they made their way to a pub that was just around the corner from the hotel. There was bound to be some music or singing; they were all thinking. But to their dismay, they found themselves the only ones in the pub. The girls sat on stools at the bar, waiting for someone to come and serve them, but no one seemed to be around.

"There is a strange feeling about this place. There is no one here to serve, no one outside, it's like a ghost town", said Mary looking around the pub.

"Oh, keep quiet Mam", said Geraldine. "You are giving me the shivers. You have been listening to too many ghost stories since we came".

They were just about to leave when a man came in from the back. "Good evening ladies, what's it to be then? I hope I haven't kept you waiting, I have just been down in the cellar".

"Will there be any music here tonight?" Catherine asked.

"No, I'm afraid not girls, sure it's very quiet here through the week, the TV has put a stop to all that. Now if you come back on Saturday night there will be plenty of music and a few set dances".

"Never mind", said Mary. "It would have been nice to see a few set dances, but we are only here for one night".

When they finished their drink, Catherine suggested they go on a pub crawl seeing there was no music. When they got to the door, they found it was pouring down with rain.

"It looks as if we are going to have to return to the hotel", said Catherine. "It looks as if it's in for the night."

Just then a man came running into the doorway out of the rain and started chatting to them.

"So you are here on holiday then?" he asked, trying to be friendly.

"Yes", replied Mary. "We were hoping to find a pub with some music, but it seems we have come at the wrong time.

"Well, I'm off to a pub at the top of the road. I am sure you will have a singsong there. Come on", he said, putting his cap on Mary's head. So, they all followed him, all of them running to get out of the heavy downpour.

The pub was nearly as quiet as the one they had just left. There were two customers, an old man sitting by a lovely old turf fire the sparks flying as he added another sod of turf and a young man sitting at the bar talking to a very pretty young barmaid. Mary went and got drinks while Catherine and Geraldine sat down at a table to shake the rain out of their hair. After they got themselves settled the man who had brought them came over and introduced himself as Kevin Lynch. He told them all about himself. He had a cattle farm just outside of town and a lovely big apple orchard. He was a bachelor and that he lived with his mother. The girls told him a little about themselves and why they were over in Ireland. They were enjoying the craic with Kevin as he was quite a comic, they were having a good laugh at the tales he was telling them, but they were sure half of them were made up because he had an audience. Before very long there was quite a crowd of people most of them were on holiday, so music was soon playing by a man playing the fiddle and his two sons playing an accordion and tin whistle. The singing soon started, and the girls loved it, then the musicians played some jigs and reels, and almost everyone was up on the floor dancing having a great time. The girls were really enjoying the night they were glad they had met Kevin as they thought that it was going to be a miserable night staying in a hotel bedroom.

At closing time, they were pleased to see it had stopped

raining. Kevin said he would walk back with them to their hotel. He said he had not enjoyed himself so much for a long time, and then he asked Mary if she would go home with him to see his orchard. The girls thought this was a great joke; they finally said goodnight to him before going into the hotel and straight up to see Bridie. They all sat on the bed to tell her all about the night out they had had and of course all about Kevin Lynch.

Bridie was pleased that they had enjoyed themselves but had to keep telling them to keep their laughter down in case they disturbed the other guests and to get back to their rooms and into bed. But Bridie smiled to herself as they left.

The girls had hangovers the next morning, all of them swearing that they would never touch a drink again. After breakfast Bridie and the girls left the hotel to make their way back to Dunclare, it was a beautiful morning, and the fresh air made them feel a lot better. It was a lovely drive back. They even stopped at Our Lady's grotto to say a few prayers in thanksgiving for a lovely holiday and reunion and a safe journey back to England. The countryside looked lovely after all the rain the night before with the warm sun drying the roads. You had a contented feeling when people passing gave a cheerful wave, also seeing the farmers taking their cattle to be milked as if they had all the time in the world, but it made them enjoy their drive back.

Tom, Danny and Eileen were pleased to see them back as Danny only had a few more days before flying back to America. Tonight, was the last night for Bridie to be with her brothers, so they had a special tea made by Eileen and the girls. Then later on in the evening, they had a few drinks and talked again about the days gone by when they were young.

The next morning the girls put their luggage into the car then kissed goodbye to their aunt and uncles leaving Bridie to say her last goodbyes to her brothers all of them knowing they would never see each other again. Bridie climbed into the car, wiping her tear-stained face as Tom, Danny and Eileen waved them out of sight with Geraldine giving a final hoot on the car as they turned the corner. The owner of the garage thanked them for bringing back the car in good condition. Then he kindly ran them to Castlerea railway station for their train to Dublin.

When they were settled on the train, Mary said, "Well Mam was it worth all the travelling? Did you enjoy yourself?"

"I loved every minute of it", Bridie said with feeling. "I was thinking to myself how my mother would have loved to have seen our Danny just one more time after he went to America and to see what a fine man he had turned out. But thank God he looks so well, so does our Tom. I'm sure Tom will live to be a hundred, he's so easy going and of course, the way that Eileen looks after him he will".

When they arrived in Dublin, they took a taxi to Drumcondra Road where they were to spend their last night at Mrs Ryan's boarding house. Mrs Ryan was a lovely woman and wanted to make tea for them, but they declined her generous offer as they were going out for dinner as this was their last night.

Bridie said she felt like a real lady going to a posh restaurant to dine. They had a lovely meal, but then they made their way back to Mrs Ryan's as the time was getting on and they did not want her to have to stay up for them coming in.

Next morning, they all felt great after a good night's sleep, then Mrs Ryan made them all a lovely breakfast then came and sat with them as she brought in another pot of tea. Mrs Ryan was a very friendly woman. She was very interested in the reason they were over in Ireland, especially about seeing her brother after so many years. Then she told them a little about herself, Mrs Ryan said she was enjoying the chat as she did not get many visitors these days. She told them that she lived in America for many years then her husband was in poor health, so they decided to come back home and bought this boarding house, but sadly her husband died two years after they came back home. Bridie and the girls could have sat longer talking to their landlady as she was very interesting, but they had to leave to get their plane. When the taxi came for them to leave Mrs Ryan gave Bridie a pound of Irish butter and a farrel of soda bread saying, "I'm sure you will enjoy this when you get back to your home in England. God bless you all". Then she stood at the door to wave them goodbye.

Chapter 13

Although Bridie would always think of Ireland as her home, she was still glad to get back to her home in Wallsend, also to see the rest of her family. Bridie's family was getting bigger. She had eighteen grandchildren whom she loved dearly, and they in return loved her as she never forgot their birthdays and Christmas presents. It never worried Bridie that she did not have a lot of money, but she was always hoping that one Saturday night she would win the pools and give it to her family.

Bridie never went far from home. She went to church on Sundays also on two afternoons a week she would go to bingo with her friends Martha Rice and Doris Bell. They would have a cup of tea and hear all the gossip before the bingo began. The family were pleased that their mother went out to bingo; she always did like a little gamble on the horses and still had her small bet each day, so her mind was always alert. Every day she would have family call, Mary, who lived nearby would call in every day, then at night, she would be quite content to watch her favourite programmes on television.

It would be Bridie's 80th birthday in July, so the family began making plans to have a party for her. There were too many in the family now to hold it in one of the houses, so Mary suggested the church hall and Father Lynch was happy for them to use it. Arrangements got started for the surprise party, all the children were sworn to secrecy, Bridie's daughters and granddaughters decorated the hall with green, white and gold streamers and balloons. They did all the cooking but had a beautiful cake made decorated with shamrocks. They invited Bridie's friends, and Sean's nephews from Scotland came. All the grandchildren some coming from as far as Canada and Belgium were there. Jane, Bridie's oldest and dearest friend, was in on the plans from the start so on the day of Bridie's birthday she called to wish her many happy returns as she did every year

"Bridie" said Jane. "There is a feis on in the hall, do you fancy coming with me? It will be nice to see the children dancing".

"Oh yes, I would love to see them. I just need to brush my hair and slip my coat on", said Bridie.

They walked the short distance to the church hall arm in arm as they always did, chatting away to each other. When they reached the hall, Jane opened the door but made sure her friend would go in first as she was greeted with a chorus of everyone singing happy birthday. She was handed a beautiful bouquet of flowers. It took Bridie a few minutes to realise what was happening. She could not believe her eyes were seeing all her family and friends. Bridie was taken to a seat and given a cup of tea. They could see she was being overwhelmed as everyone crowded around her, all wanting to wish her happy birthday.

Afterwards, she enjoyed watching her family dancing jigs and reels with the grandchildren. Everyone had a good time saying they should have a family party more often as it was only on a rare occasion now that they all got together. Bridie was so proud of all her family. She was also happy that they were proud of their Irish heritage. It was evening when everyone started to go home quite tired. The family were so pleased that the party had gone off so well. It also showed Bridie how much she was loved by all her family and friends.

Time goes by so fast, but the family never thought of their mother being old, she was now eighty-three years of age, but her mind was still very alert, reading three or four books in a week. She could still converse too about politics and religion or the latest news on the television or in the newspapers. She could still beat any of the family at spelling or arithmetic and still had a good hand for writing. Bridie still liked nothing better than her little gamble, apart from going to bingo a couple of afternoons, she still had her daily bet on the horses, always putting her couple of shilling on an Irish horse of course. She could reckon up in seconds how much she would get back if she had a winner. She enjoyed a Saturday evening when some of the family went to her house to have a game of cards.

It was in the winter of 1985 Bridie's family noticed that her appetite was poor, so she had lost weight. They were getting worried about her. She lost all interest in going to bingo making up all kinds of excuses but eventually admitted she was having some pain in her stomach. The doctor gave Bridie tablets to take, after a few days she said she was feeling a lot better.

Jane, Bridie's best friend, still called every day to have a cup of tea and chat, so Bridie missed her very much when Jane went into the hospital. Bridie asked her son Patrick to take her to the hospital to see Jane. Jane was really pleased to see them but scolded her friend for coming when she was ill herself. After half an hour, Patrick decided it was time for his mother to be home and in bed herself. Bridie kissed Jane goodbye saying she would see her when she came home in a couple of days.

The next couple of weeks, Bridie sat in her armchair by

the fireside saying it was far too cold to be going out, but she always had a smile and a welcome for anyone who called. Bridie missed Jane very much as she had gone back to Lurgan with her cousins to recuperate. Mary, who lived near to her mother called in two or three times each day to see her. When she went to see her one day, she found her mother still in bed, she knew her mother must be ill as she would never take to her bed any time during the day. Mary asked her mother if she felt ill, Bridie answered saying, "There is nothing wrong with me. I was just a little tired that's all".

Bridie made an attempt to get out of bed but could not make it. Mary, who was quite worried about her mother, asked if she had any pain, Bridie denied it at first but then had to admit that she terrible pain in her stomach.

Oh my God, it must be serious thought Mary shaking as she phoned the doctor, then phoned her brother Pat and sisters Margaret and Catherine. They were all with their mother when the doctor arrived. The doctor said that Bridie had to go into the hospital to check what could be wrong; she then phoned for an ambulance. Patrick said he would go in the ambulance with his mother as they carried her in on a stretcher. Even though Bridie was ill, she said to the girls to give the ambulance men a couple of pounds for a drink. But that was Bridie all over, always thinking of others before herself. The men shook their heads in amazement and gratefully accepted the money that Margaret gave them. That same evening Bridie underwent an operation. Afterwards, she was taken into intensive care; the family were told that it was just a precaution.

Over the following week, there was always at least two of the family at their mother's bedside. The local priest came, also, all of her grandchildren, some coming a great distance to see their beloved 'Nanna'. The doctors and nurses were amazed than an old lady was loved by so many people, they even provided a separate waiting room to accommodate them. Bridie was aware of them all coming to see her. The grandchildren all loved their 'Nanna'. She had taken care of all of them at some point, so they were all extremely close to her and were all concerned about their dear 'Nanna'.

It was a week after the operation when the doctor said Bridie was well enough to go back into the ward. Mary and Catherine saw that their mother was settled before leaving the hospital a lot happier after all the worry and stress they had been through over the last week. When Mary arrived home, there was a letter from Jane's cousin in Ireland saying that Jane had died peacefully in her sleep. They were to make arrangements for her body to be flown back to Newcastle to be buried beside Dick, her late husband in Wallsend. Mary just sat down and cried. She had been through a terrible week with all the worry over her mother and now poor Jane, a

 special friend of her mother was now dead. The rest of the family were informed about Jane's death, and they all agreed they would not tell their mother until she was fully recovered and back home again.

Early the following morning, the loud ringing of the phone awoke Mary out of her much-needed sleep. Mary's heart was pounding in her chest as she jumped out of bed to answer it. Patrick had rung her to say he had just received a call from the hospital; their mother had taken ill and could possibly slip into a coma. He had phoned a taxi to take them to the hospital.

Bridie was still conscious when they arrived. Their mother was still able to smile and say a few words to her family; she also thanked the priest for coming. It was late afternoon with her family at her bedside that Bridie fell asleep never to wake again, leaving behind her broken-hearted family.

The day Bridie died, she left many sad people who she had given so much love and understanding. Her Irish culture will always live on through her family and grandchildren.

Bridie you were a wonderful mother just as your mother Maggie said that you would be all those years ago in your house in Dunclare.

For I should know, as you were my mother.

Mary

X

Printed in Great Britain
by Amazon

63402825R00078